D0021506

Diary of a Bad Year

J. M. Coetzee

Diary of a Bad Year

VIKING

VIKING
Published by the Penguin Group
Penguin Group (USA) Inc., 375 Hudson Street,
New York, New York 10014, U.S.A.
Penguin Group (Canada), 90 Eglinton Avenue East, Suite 700,
Toronto, Ontario, Canada M4P 2Y3
(a division of Pearson Penguin Canada Inc.)
Penguin Books Ltd, 80 Strand, London WC2R 0RL, England
Penguin Ireland, 25 St. Stephen's Green, Dublin 2, Ireland
(a division of Penguin Books Ltd)
Penguin Books Australia Ltd, 250 Camberwell Road, Camberwell,
Victoria 3124, Australia
(a division of Pearson Australia Group Pty Ltd)
Penguin Books India Pvt Ltd, 11 Community Centre, Panchsheel Park,
New Delhi – 110 017, India
Penguin Group (NZ), 67 Apollo Drive, Rosedale, North Shore 0632,
New Zealand (a division of Pearson New Zealand Ltd.)
Penguin Books (South Africa) (Pty) Ltd, 24 Sturdee Avenue,
Rosebank, Johannesburg 2196, South Africa

Penguin Books Ltd, Registered Offices:
80 Strand, London WC2R 0RL, England

First American edition
Published in 2008 by Viking Penguin,
a member of Penguin Group (USA) Inc.

10 9 8 7 6 5 4 3 2 1

A portion of this book first appeared in *The New York Review of Books*.

Publisher's Note
This is a work of fiction. Names, characters, places, and incidents either are the product of the author's imagination or are used fictitiously, and any resemblance to actual persons, living or dead, business establishments, events, or locales is entirely coincidental.

LIBRARY OF CONGRESS CATALOGING IN PUBLICATION DATA

Coetzee, J. M., 1940–
Diary of a bad year / J.M. Coetzee.
p. cm.
ISBN 978-0-670-01875-8
I. Title.
PR9369.3.C58D48 2007
823'.912—dc22
                          2007027378

Printed in the United States of America

Contents

One

Strong Opinions

12 September 2005 – 31 May 2006

01. On the origins of the state

Every account of the origins of the state starts from the premise that "we" – not we the readers but some generic we so wide as to exclude no one – participate in its coming into being. But the fact is that the only "we" we know – ourselves and the people close to us – are born into the state; and our forebears too were born into the state as far back as we can trace. The state is always there before we are.

(How far back can we trace? In African thought, the consensus is that after the seventh generation we can no longer distinguish between history and myth.)

If, despite the evidence of our senses, we accept the premise that we or our forebears created the state, then we must also accept its entailment: that we or our forebears could have created the state in some other form, if we had chosen; perhaps, too, that we could change it if we collectively so decided. But the fact is that, even collectively, those who are "under" the state, who "belong to" the state, will find it very hard indeed to change its form; they – we – are certainly powerless to abolish it.

It is hardly in our power to change the form of the state and impossible to abolish it because, vis-à-vis the state, we are, precisely, powerless. In the myth of the founding of the state as set down by Thomas Hobbes, our descent into powerlessness was voluntary: in order to escape the violence of internecine warfare without end (reprisal upon reprisal, vengeance upon vengeance, the vendetta), we individually and severally yielded up to the state the right to use physical force (right is might, might is right), thereby entering the realm (the protection) of the law. Those who chose and choose to stay outside the compact become outlaw.

My first glimpse of her was in the laundry room. It was mid-morning on a quiet spring day and I was sitting, watching the washing go around, when this quite startling young woman walked in. Startling because the last thing I was expecting was such an apparition; also because the tomato-red shift she wore was so startling in its brevity.

The law protects the law-abiding citizen. It even protects to a degree the citizen who, without denying the force of the law, nevertheless uses force against his fellow citizen: the punishment prescribed for the offender must be condign with his offence. Even the enemy soldier, inasmuch as he is the representative of a rival state, shall not be put to death if captured. But there is no law to protect the outlaw, the man who takes up arms against his own state, that is to say, the state that claims him as its own.

Outside the state (the commonwealth, the *statum civitatis*), says Hobbes, the individual may feel he enjoys perfect liberty, but that liberty does him no good. Within the state, on the other hand, "every citizen retains as much liberty as he needs to live well in peace, [while] enough liberty is taken from others to remove the fear of them . . . To sum up: outside the commonwealth is the empire of passions, war, fear, poverty, nastiness, solitude, barbarity, ignorance, savagery; within the commonwealth is the empire of reason, peace, security, wealth, splendour, society, good taste, the sciences and good-will."[1]

What the Hobbesian myth of origins does not mention is that the handover of power to the state is irreversible. The option is not open to us to change our minds, to decide that the monopoly on the exercise of force held by the state, codified in the law, is not what we wanted after all, that we would prefer to go back to a state of nature.

We are born subject. From the moment of our birth we are subject. One mark of this subjection is the certificate of birth. The perfected state holds and guards the monopoly of certifying birth. Either you are given (and carry with you) the certificate of the state, thereby acquiring an *identity* which during the course of your life enables the state to identify you and track you (track you down); or you do without an identity and condemn yourself to living outside the state like an animal (animals do not have identity papers).

The spectacle of me may have given her a start too: a crumpled old fellow in a corner who at first glance might have been a tramp off the street. Hello, she said coolly, and then went about her business, which was to empty two white canvas bags into a top-loader, bags in which male underwear seemed to predominate.

Not only may you not enter the state without certification: you are, in the eyes of the state, not dead until you are certified dead; and you can be certified dead only by an officer who himself (herself) holds state certification. The state pursues the certification of death with extraordinary thoroughness – witness the dispatch of a host of forensic scientists and bureaucrats to scrutinize and photograph and prod and poke the mountain of human corpses left behind by the great tsunami of December 2004 in order to establish their individual identities. No expense is spared to ensure that the census of subjects shall be complete and accurate.

Whether the citizen lives or dies is not a concern of the state. What matters to the state and its records is whether the citizen is alive or dead.

*

The Seven Samurai is a film in complete command of its medium yet naïve enough to deal simply and directly with first things. Specifically it deals with the birth of the state, and it does so with Shakespearean clarity and comprehensiveness. In fact, what *The Seven Samurai* offers is no less than the Kurosawan theory of the origin of the state.

Nice day, I said. Yes, she said, with her back to me. Are you new? I said, meaning was she new to Sydenham Towers, though other meanings were possible too, *Are you new on this earth?* for example. No, she said. How it creaks, getting a conversation going. I live on the ground floor, I said. I am allowed to make gambits like that, it will be put down to garrulity. Such a garrulous old man, she will remark to the owner of the pink shirt with the white collar, I had a hard time getting away from him, one doesn't want to be rude. I live on the ground floor and have since 1995 and still I don't know all my neighbours, I said. Yeah, she said, and no more, meaning, *Yes, I hear what you say and I agree, it is tragic not to know who your neighbours are, but that is how it is in the big city and I have other things to attend to now, so could we let the present exchange of pleasantries die a natural death?*

The story told in the film is of a village during a time of political disorder – a time when the state has in effect ceased to exist – and of the relations of the villagers with a troop of armed bandits. After years of descending upon the village like a storm, raping the women, killing those men who resist, and bearing away stored-up food supplies, the bandits hit on the idea of systematizing their visits, calling on the village just once a year to exact or extort tribute (tax). That is to say, the bandits cease being predators upon the village and become parasites instead.

One presumes that the bandits have other such "pacified" villages under their thumb, that they descend upon them in rotation, that in ensemble such villages constitute the bandits' tax base. Very likely they have to fight off rival bands for control of specific villages, although we see none of this in the film.

The bandits have not yet begun to live among their subjects, having their wants taken care of day by day – that is to say, they have not yet turned the villagers into a slave population. Kurosawa is thus laying out for our consideration a very early stage in the growth of the state.

The main action of the film starts when the villagers conceive a plan of hiring their own band of hard men, the seven unemployed samurai of the title, to protect them from the bandits. The plan works, the bandits are defeated (the body of the film is taken up with skirmishes and battles), the samurai are victorious. Having seen how the protection and extortion system works, the samurai band, the new parasites, make an offer to the villagers: they will, at a price, take the village under their wing, that is to say, will take the place of the bandits. But in a rather wishful ending the villagers decline: they ask the samurai to leave, and the samurai comply.

She has black black hair, shapely bones. A certain golden glow to her skin, *lambent* might be the word. As for the bright red shift, that is perhaps not the item of attire she would have chosen if she were expecting strange male company in the laundry room at eleven in the morning on a weekday. Red shift and thongs. Thongs of the kind that go on the feet.

The Kurosawan story of the origins of the state is still played out in our times in Africa, where gangs of armed men grab power – that is to say, annex the national treasury and the mechanisms of taxing the population – do away with their rivals, and proclaim Year One. Though these African military gangs are often no larger or more powerful than the organized criminal gangs of Asia or eastern Europe, their activities are respectfully covered in the media – even the Western media – under the heading of politics (world affairs) rather than crime.

One can cite examples of the birth or rebirth of the state from Europe too. In the vacuum of power left by the defeat of the armies of the Third Reich in 1944–5, rival armed gangs scrambled to take charge of the newly liberated nations; who took power where was determined by who could call on what foreign army for backing.

Did anyone, in 1944, say to the French populace: *Consider: the retreat of our German overlords means that for a brief moment we are ruled by no one. Do we want to end that moment, or do we perhaps want to perpetuate it – to become the first people in modern times to roll back the state? Let us, as French people, use our new and sudden freedom to debate the question without restraint.* Perhaps some poet spoke the words; but if he did his voice must at once have been silenced by the armed gangs, who in this case and in all cases have more in common with each other than with the people.

*

As I watched her an ache, a metaphysical ache, crept over me that I did nothing to stem. And in an intuitive way she knew about it, knew that in the old man in the plastic chair in the corner there was something personal going on, something to do with age and regret and the tears of things. Which she did not particularly like, did not want to evoke, though it was a tribute to her, to her beauty and freshness as well as to the shortness of her dress. Had it come from someone different, had it had a simpler and blunter meaning, she might have been readier to give it a welcome; but from an old man its meaning was too diffuse and melancholy for a nice day when you are in a hurry to get the chores done.

In the days of kings, the subject was told: *You used to be the subject of King A, now King A is dead and behold, you are the subject of King B.* Then democracy arrived, and the subject was for the first time presented with a choice: *Do you (collectively) want to be ruled by Citizen A or Citizen B?*

Always the subject is presented with the accomplished fact: in the first case with the fact of his subjecthood, in the second with the fact of the choice. The form of the choice is not open to discussion. The ballot paper does not say: *Do you want A or B or neither?* It certainly never says: *Do you want A or B or no one at all?* The citizen who expresses his unhappiness with the form of choice on offer by the only means open to him – not voting, or else spoiling his ballot paper – is simply not counted, that is to say, is discounted, ignored.

Faced with a choice between A and B, given the kind of A and the kind of B who usually make it onto the ballot paper, most people, *ordinary* people, are in their hearts inclined to choose neither. But that is only an inclination, and the state does not deal in inclinations. Inclinations are not part of the currency of politics. What the state deals in are choices. The ordinary person would like to say: *Some days I incline to A, some days to B, most days I just feel they should both go away;* or else, *Some of A and some of B, sometimes, and at other times neither A nor B but something quite different.* The state shakes its head. *You have to choose,* says the state: *A or B.*

*

A week passed before I saw her again – in a well-designed apartment block like this, tracking one's neighbours is not easy – and then only fleetingly as she passed through the front door in a flash of white slacks that showed off a derrière so near to perfect as to be angelic. God, grant me one wish before I die, I whispered; but then was overtaken with shame at the specificity of the wish, and withdrew it.

"Spreading democracy," as is now being done by the United States in the Middle East, means spreading the rules of democracy. It means telling people that whereas formerly they had no choice, now they have a choice. Formerly they had A and nothing but A; now they have a choice between A and B. "Spreading freedom" means creating the conditions for people to choose freely between A and B. The spreading of freedom and the spreading of democracy go hand in hand. The people engaged in spreading freedom and democracy see no irony in the description of the process just given.

During the Cold War, the explanation given by Western democratic states for the banning of their Communist parties was that a party whose stated aim is the destruction of the democratic process should not be allowed to participate in the democratic process, defined as choosing between A and B.

*

Why is it so hard to say anything about politics from outside politics? Why can there be no discourse about politics that is not itself political? To Aristotle the answer is that politics is built into human nature, that is, is part of our fate, as monarchy is the fate of bees. To strive for a systematic, supra-political discourse about politics is futile.

From Vinnie, who looks after the North Tower, I learn that she – whom I am prudent enough to describe not as *the young woman in the alluringly short shift and now in the elegant white slacks*, but as *the young woman with the dark hair* – is the wife or at least girlfriend of the pale, hurrying, plump and ever-sweaty fellow whose path crosses mine now and again in the lobby and for whom my private name is Mr Aberdeen; further, that she is not new in the customary sense of the word, having (together with Mr A) occupied since January a prime unit on the top floor of this same North Tower.

02. On anarchism

When the phrase "the bastards" is used in Australia, its reference is understood on all sides. "The bastards" was once the convict's term for the men who called themselves his betters and flogged him if he disagreed. Now "the bastards" are the politicians, the men and women who run the state. The problem: how to assert the legitimacy of the old perspective, the perspective from below, the convict's perspective, when it is of the nature of that perspective to be illegitimate, *against* the law, *against* the bastards.

Opposition to the bastards, opposition to government in general under the banner of libertarianism, has acquired a bad name because all too often its roots lie in a reluctance to pay taxes. Whatever one's views on paying tribute to the bastards, a strategic first step must be to distinguish oneself from that particular libertarian strain. How to do so? "Take half of what I own, take half of what I earn, I yield it to you; in return, leave me alone." Would that be enough to prove one's bona fides?

Michel de Montaigne's young friend Etienne de La Boétie, writing in 1549, saw the passivity of populations vis-à-vis their rulers as first an acquired and then later an inherited vice, an obstinate "will to be ruled" that becomes so deep-rooted "that even the love of liberty comes to seem not quite as natural."

Thank you, I said to Vinnie. In an ideal world I might have thought of a way to interrogate him further (Which unit? Under what name?) without unseemliness. But this is not an ideal world.

Her connection with the no doubt freckle-backed Mr Aberdeen is a great disappointment. It pains me to think of the two of them side by side, that is to say, side by side in bed, since that is what counts, finally. Not just because of the insult – the insult to natural justice – of such a dull man in possession of so celestial a paramour, but because of what the fruit of their union might look like, her golden glow quite washed out by his Celtic pallor.

It is incredible to see how the populace, once they have been subjected, fall suddenly into such profound forgetfulness of their earlier independence that it becomes impossible for them to rouse themselves and recover it; in fact, they proceed to serve so much without prompting, so freely, that one would say, on the face of it, they have not lost their liberty but won their servitude. It may be true that, to begin with, one serves because one has to, because one is constrained to by force; but those who come later serve without regret, and perform of their own free will what their predecessors performed under constraint. So it happens that men, born under the yoke, brought up in servitude, are content to live as they were born . . . assuming as their natural state the conditions under which they were born.[2]

Well said. Nevertheless, in an important respect La Boétie gets it wrong. The alternatives are not placid servitude on the one hand and revolt against servitude on the other. There is a third way, chosen by thousands and millions of people every day. It is the way of quietism, of willed obscurity, of inner emigration.

Days could be spent in devising felicitous coincidences to allow the brief exchange in the laundry room to be picked up elsewhere. But life is too short for plotting. So let me simply say that the second intersection of our paths took place in a public park, the park across the street, where I spotted her taking her ease under an extravagantly large sun hat, browsing through a magazine. She was in a more amiable mood this time, less curt with me; I was able to confirm from her own lips that she was for the present without significant occupation, or, as she put it, *between jobs*: hence the sun hat, hence the magazine, hence the languor of her days. Her previous employment, she said, had been in the hospitality industry; she would in due course (but there was no hurry) be seeking redeployment in the same field.

03. On democracy

The main problem in the life of the state is the problem of succession: how to ensure that power will be passed from one set of hands to the next without a contest of arms.

In comfortable times we forget how terrible civil war is, how rapidly it descends into mindless slaughter. René Girard's fable of the warring twins is pertinent: the fewer the substantive differences between the two parties, the more bitter their mutual hatred. One recalls Daniel Defoe's comment on religious strife in England: that adherents of the national church would swear to their detestation of Papists and Popery not knowing whether the Pope was a man or a horse.

Early solutions to the problem of succession have a distinctly arbitrary look: on the ruler's death, his firstborn male child will succeed to power, for example. The advantage of the firstborn male solution is that the firstborn male is unique; the disadvantage is that the firstborn male in question may have no aptitude to rule. The annals of kingdoms are rife with stories of incompetent princes, to say nothing of kings unable to father sons.

From a practical point of view, it does not matter how succession is managed as long as it does not precipitate the country into civil war. A scheme in which many (though usually only two) candidates for leadership present themselves to the populace and subject themselves to a ballot is only one of a score that an inventive mind might come up with. It is not the scheme itself that matters, but consensus to adopt the scheme and abide by the results.

All the while she was conveying this rather desultory information the air around us positively crackled with a current that could not have come from me, I do not exude currents any more, must therefore have come from her and been aimed at no one in particular, just released into the environment. Hospitality, she repeated, or else perhaps human resources, she had some experience in human resources (whatever those might be) too; and again the shadow of the ache passed over me, the ache I alluded to earlier, of a metaphysical or at least post-physical kind.

Thus in itself succession by the firstborn is neither better nor worse than succession by democratic election. But to live in democratic times means to live in times when only the democratic scheme has currency and prestige.

As during the time of kings it would have been naïve to think that the king's firstborn son would be the fittest to rule, so in our time it is naïve to think that the democratically elected ruler will be the fittest. The rule of succession is not a formula for identifying the best ruler, it is a formula for conferring legitimacy on someone or other and thus forestalling civil conflict. The electorate – the *demos* – believes that its task is to choose the best man, but in truth its task is much simpler: to anoint a man (*vox populi vox dei*), it does not matter whom. Counting ballots may seem to be a means of finding which is the true (that is, the loudest) *vox populi*; but the power of the ballot-count formula, like the power of the formula of the firstborn male, lies in the fact that it is objective, unambiguous, outside the field of political contestation. The toss of a coin would be equally objective, equally unambiguous, equally incontestable, and could therefore equally well be claimed (as it has been claimed) to represent *vox dei*. We do not choose our rulers by the toss of a coin – tossing coins is associated with the low-status activity of gambling – but who would dare to claim that the world would be in a worse state than it is if rulers had from the beginning of time been chosen by the method of the coin?

In the meantime, she went on, I help Alan with reports and so forth, so he can claim me as a secretarial resource.

Alan, I said.

I imagine, as I write these words, that I am arguing this anti-democratic case to a sceptical reader who will continually be comparing my claims with the facts on the ground: does what I say about democracy square with the facts about democratic Australia, the democratic United States, and so forth? The reader should bear it in mind that for every democratic Australia there are two Byelorussias or Chads or Fijis or Colombias that likewise subscribe to the formula of the ballot-count.

Australia is by most standards an advanced democracy. It is also a land where cynicism about politics and contempt for politicians abound. But such cynicism and contempt are quite comfortably accommodated within the system. If you have reservations about the system and want to change it, the democratic argument goes, do so within the system: put yourself forward as a candidate for political office, subject yourself to the scrutiny and the vote of fellow citizens. Democracy does not allow for politics outside the democratic system. In this sense, democracy is totalitarian.

If you take issue with democracy in times when everyone claims to be heart and soul a democrat, you run the risk of losing touch with reality. To regain touch, you must at every moment remind yourself of what it is like to come face to face with the state – the democratic state or any other – in the person of the state official. Then ask yourself: Who serves whom? Who is the servant, who the master?

Alan, she said, my partner. And she gave me a look. The look did not say, *Yes, I am to all intents and purposes a married woman, so if you pursue the course you have in mind it will be a matter of clandestine adultery, with all the risks and thrills pertaining thereto,* nothing like that, on the contrary it said, *You seem to think I am some sort of child, do I need to point out I am not a child at all?*

I too am in need of a secretary, I said, grasping the nettle.

Yes? she said.

04. On Machiavelli

On talkback radio ordinary members of the public have been calling in to say that, while they concede that torture is in general a bad thing, it may nonetheless sometimes be necessary. Some even advance the proposition that we may have to do evil for the sake of a greater good. In general they are scornful of absolutist opponents of torture: such people, they say, do not have their feet on the ground, do not live in the real world.

Machiavelli says that if as a ruler you accept that your every action must pass moral scrutiny, you will without fail be defeated by an opponent who submits to no such moral test. To hold on to power, you have not only to master the crafts of deception and treachery but to be prepared to use them where necessary.

Necessity, *necessità*, is Machiavelli's guiding principle. The old, pre-Machiavellian position was that the moral law was supreme. If it so happened that the moral law was sometimes broken, that was unfortunate, but rulers were merely human, after all. The new, Machiavellian position is that infringing the moral law is justified when it is necessary.

Thus is inaugurated the dualism of modern political culture, which simultaneously upholds absolute and relative standards of value. The modern state appeals to morality, to religion, and to natural law as the ideological foundation of its existence. At the same time it is prepared to infringe any or all of these in the interest of self-preservation.

Yes, I said, I happen to be a writer by profession, and I have a major deadline to meet, as a consequence of which I need someone to type a manuscript for me and perhaps do a little editing as well and generally make the whole thing shipshape.

She looked blank.

Neat and orderly and readable, I mean, I said.

Use someone from a bureau, she said. There is a bureau on King Street that Alan's company uses when they have urgent work.

Machiavelli does not deny that the claims morality makes on us are absolute. *At the same time* he asserts that in the interest of the state the ruler "is often obliged [*necessitato*] to act without loyalty, without mercy, without humanity, and without religion."[3]

The kind of person who calls talkback radio and justifies the use of torture in the interrogation of prisoners holds the double standard in his mind in exactly the same way: without in the least denying the absolute claims of the Christian ethic (love thy neighbour as thyself), such a person approves freeing the hands of the authorities – the army, the secret police – to do whatever may be necessary to protect the public from enemies of the state.

The typical reaction of liberal intellectuals is to seize on the contradiction here: how can something be both wrong and right, or at least both wrong and OK, at the same time? What liberal intellectuals fail to see is that this so-called contradiction expresses the quintessence of the Machiavellian and therefore the modern, a quintessence that has been thoroughly absorbed by the man in the street. The world is ruled by necessity, says the man in the street, not by some abstract moral code. We have to do what we have to do.

If you wish to counter the man in the street, it cannot be by appeal to moral principles, much less by demanding that people should run their lives in such a way that there are no contradictions between what they say and what they do. Ordinary life is full of contradictions; ordinary people are used to accommodating them. Rather, you must attack the metaphysical, supra-empirical status of *necessità* and show that to be fraudulent.

I don't need someone from a bureau, I said. I need someone who can pick up instalments and get them back to me speedily. That person should also have a feel, an intuitive feel, for what I am trying to do. Can I perhaps interest you in the work, since we are near neighbours and since you are, as you say, between jobs? I will pay, I said, and I mentioned a rate per hour which, even if she had once been the tsarina of hospitality, must have given her pause to reflect. Because of the urgency, I said. Because of the looming deadline.

05. On terrorism

The Australian parliament is about to enact anti-terrorist legislation whose effect will be to suspend a range of civil liberties indefinitely into the future. The word *hysterical* has been used to describe the response to terror attacks by the governments of the United States, Britain, and now Australia. It is not a bad word, not undescriptive, but it has no explanatory power. Why should our rulers, normally phlegmatic men, react with sudden hysteria to the pin-pricks of terrorism when for decades they were able to go about their everyday business unruffled, in full awareness that in a deep bunker somewhere in the Urals an enemy watched and waited with a finger on a button, ready if provoked to wipe them and their cities from the face of the earth?

One explanation on offer is that the new foe is irrational. The old Soviet foes might have been cunning and even devilish, but they were not irrational. They played the game of nuclear diplomacy as they played the game of chess: the so-called nuclear option might be included in their repertoire of moves, but the decision to take it would ultimately be rational (decision-making based on probability theory being counted here as eminently rational, though by its very nature it involves making gambles, taking chances), as would decisions made in the West. Therefore the game would be played by the same rules on both sides.

An intuitive feel: those were my words. They were a gamble, a shot in the dark, but they worked. What self-respecting woman would want to deny she has an intuitive feel? Thus has it come about that my opinions, in all their drafts and revisions, are to pass under the eye and through the hands of Anya (her name), of Alan and Anya, A & A, unit 2514, even though the Anya in question has never done a stitch of editing in her life and even though Bruno Geistler of Mittwoch Verlag GmbH has people on his staff perfectly capable of turning dictaphone tapes in English into a shipshape manuscript in German.

This new contest, however (so proceeds the explanation), is not being played by the rules of rationality. The Russians made survival (national survival, which in politics means the survival of the state and in the game of international chess the ability to go on playing) their least negotiable demand. The Islamist terrorists, on the other hand, care nothing about survival, either at the individual level (this life is as nothing compared with the life after death) or at the national level (Islam is larger than the nation; God will not allow Islam to be defeated). Nor do such terrorists follow the rationalist calculus of costs and benefits: to deal a blow to God's enemies is enough, the cost of that blow, material or human, is unimportant.

Thus runs one account of why the "war on terror" is an unusual kind of war. But there is a second account too, one that does not get so wide an airing, namely that since terrorists are the equivalent not of an opposing army but of an armed criminal gang representing no state and claiming no national home, the conflict in which they engage us is categorically different from the conflict between states and must be played by a quite different set of rules. "We do not negotiate with terrorists, as we do not negotiate with criminals."

The state has always been very touchy on the subject of whom it treats with. To the state, the only contracts that count as valid are contracts with other states. How the rulers of those states came to power is of secondary importance. Once "recognized," any rival ruler will qualify as a co-player, a member of the league.

I stood up. I will leave you now, I said, to get on with your reading. If I had had a hat I would have doffed it, it would have been the right old-world gesture for the occasion.

Don't go yet, she said. Tell me first, what sort of book is this going to be?

What I am in the process of putting together is strictly speaking not a book, I said, but a contribution to a book.

The prevailing rules for who may play the game of war and who may not are self-interested rules, drawn up by national governments and in no case I am aware of placed before the citizenry for approval. In effect they define diplomacy, including the use of military force as the ultimate diplomatic measure, as a matter solely between governments. Infractions of this meta-rule are penalized with extraordinary severity. Hence Guantanamo Bay, which is more a spectacle than a prisoner-of-war camp: an awful display of what can happen to men who choose to play outside the rules of the game.

Included in the new Australian legislation is a law against speaking favourably of terrorism. It is a curb on freedom of speech, and does not pretend to be otherwise.

What intelligent person would want to speak well of Islamist terrorists – of rigid, self-righteous young men who blow themselves up in public places in order to kill people they define as enemies of the faith? No one, of course. So why be concerned at the ban, except in the abstract, as an abstract infringement of free speech? For two reasons. One, because, though dropping bombs from high altitude upon a sleeping village is no less an act of terror than blowing oneself up in a crowd, it is perfectly legal to speak well of aerial bombing ("Shock and Awe"). Two, because the situation of the suicide bomber is not without tragic potential. Whose heart is so hardened as to feel no sympathy at all for the man who, his family having been killed in an Israeli strike, straps on the bomb-belt in full knowledge that there is no paradise of houris waiting for him, and in grief and rage goes out to destroy as many of the killers as he can? *No other way than death* is a marker and perhaps even a definition of the tragic.

The book itself is the brainchild of a publisher in Germany. Its title will be *Strong Opinions*. The plan is for six contributors from various countries to say their say on any subjects they choose, the more contentious the better. Six eminent writers pronounce on what is wrong with today's world. It is due to appear in German in the middle of next year. Hence the tight deadline. The French rights are already sold, but not the English, as far as I know.

In the 1990s, I recall, I published a collection of essays on censorship. It made little impression. One reviewer dismissed it as irrelevant to the new era just dawning, the era inaugurated by the fall of the Berlin Wall and the break-up of the USSR. With world-wide liberal democracy just around the corner, he said, the state will have no reason for interfering with our freedom to write and speak as we wish; and anyhow, the new electronic media will make the surveillance and control of communications impossible to carry out.

Well, what do we see today, in 2005? Not only the re-emergence of old-fashioned restrictions of the baldest sort on freedom of speech – witness legislation in the United States, the UK, and now Australia – but surveillance (by shadowy agencies) of the entire world's tele-phonic and electronic communications. It's déjà vu all over again.

There are to be no more secrets, say the new theorists of surveil-lance, meaning something quite interesting: that the era in which secrets counted, in which secrets could exert their power over the lives of people (think of the role of secrets in Dickens, in Henry James) is over; nothing worth knowing cannot be uncovered in a matter of seconds, and without much effort; private life is, to all intents and purposes, a thing of the past.

And what is wrong with today's world? she said.

I cannot say yet what will come at the head of our list – I mean, of the list the six of us will jointly compile – but if you press me my guess is that we will say the world is unfair. An unfair dispensation, an unfair state of affairs, that is what we will say. Here we are, six *éminences grises* who have clawed our way up the highest peak, and now that we have reached the summit what do we find? We find that we are too old and infirm to enjoy the proper fruits of our triumph. *Is this all?* we say to ourselves, surveying the world of delights we cannot have. *Was it worth all that sweat?*

What is striking about such a claim is not so much its arrogance as what it inadvertently reveals about the conception of a secret that prevails in official quarters: that a secret is an item of information, and as such falls under the wing of information science, one of whose branches is *mining*, the extraction of scintillae of information (secrets) from tons of data.

The masters of information have forgotten about poetry, where words may have a meaning quite different from what the lexicon says, where the metaphoric spark is always one jump ahead of the decoding function, where another, unforeseen reading is always possible.

That is as much as I said to Anya on that occasion. What I did not mention, because it did me no honour, was that when Bruno made his proposal I jumped to accept. Yes, I will do it, I said; yes, I will meet your deadline. An opportunity to grumble in public, an opportunity to take magic revenge on the world for declining to conform to my fantasies: how could I refuse?

*

06. On guidance systems

There were times during the Cold War when the Russians fell so far behind the Americans in weapons technology that, if it had come to all-out nuclear warfare, they would have been annihilated without achieving much in the way of retaliation. During such periods, the *mutual* in Mutual Assured Destruction was in effect a fiction.

These interruptions in equilibrium came about because the Americans from time to time made leaps ahead in telemetry, navigation, and guidance systems. The Russians might possess powerful rockets and numerous warheads, but their capacity to deliver them accurately to their targets was always much inferior to that of the Americans.

As a typist pure and simple, Anya from upstairs is a bit of a disappointment. She meets her daily quota, no problem about that, but the rapport I had hoped for, the feel for the sort of thing I write, is hardly there. There are times when I stare in dismay at the text she turns in. According to Daniel Defoe, I read, the true-born Englishman hates "papers and papery." Brezhnev's generals sit "somewhere in the urinals."

As I pass him, carrying the laundry basket, I make sure I waggle my behind, my delicious behind, sheathed in tight denim. If I were a man I would not be able to keep my eyes off me. Alan says there are as many different bums in the world as there are faces. Mirror, mirror on the wall, I say to Alan, whose is the fairest of them all? Yours, my princess, my queen, yours without a doubt.

In spite of this, at no time did the Russians threaten that they would use volunteer pilots to crash aircraft carrying nuclear bombs into targets in America, sacrificing their lives in the act. There may in fact have been such volunteers; but the Russians did not claim to be holding them in reserve, or to be basing their war plans on suicide tactics.

In their later space ventures, both sides took pains to bring back to earth the astronauts or cosmonauts they launched into space, even though volunteers prepared to lay down their lives for the greater glory of the nation could certainly have been found (neither side had qualms about sending mice, dogs, or monkeys on suicide missions). The Russians might well have had cosmonauts on the moon before 1969, had they been prepared to let them die a slow death there after planting the flag.

I type what I hear, then I hand it over to spellcheck, she offers by way of explanation. Maybe spellcheck gets it wrong sometimes, but it is better than guessing.

All he writes about is politics – he, El Señor, not Alan. It's a big disappointment. It makes me yawn. I try to tell him to give it up, people have had it up to here with politics. There is no shortage of other things to write about. He could write about cricket, for example – give his personal perspective on it. I know he watches cricket. When we come in late at night, Alan and I, there he is, slumped in front of the television, you can see him from the street, he never closes the blinds.

This attitude toward the sacrifice of human life is curious. Military commanders do not think twice about ordering troops into battle in the certain knowledge that numbers of them will die. Soldiers who disobey orders and refuse to go into battle are punished, even executed. On the other hand, the officer ethos dictates that it is unacceptable to single out individual soldiers and order them to give up their lives, for example by carrying explosives into the midst of the enemy and blowing themselves up. Yet – even more paradoxically – soldiers who on their own initiative commit such acts are treated as heroes.

Toward the Japanese *kamikaze* pilots of World War Two the West has retained a degree of ambivalence. These young men were certainly brave, runs the orthodox line; nevertheless, they cannot qualify as authentic heroes because, although they sacrificed their lives and may even in a sense have volunteered to sacrifice their lives, they were psychologically embedded within a military and national ethos that held the individual life cheap. Volunteering for suicide missions was thus a kind of cultural reflex rather than a proper decision, autonomous, freely given. *Kamikaze* pilots were no more authentically heroic than bees that instinctively give up their lives to protect the hive.

Spellcheck has no mind of its own, I say. If you are prepared to hand it over to spellcheck to run your life, you might as well throw dice.

I am not averse to cricket myself, in short stretches. It's nice to see white pants stretched tight across a young male bottom. What a pair we would make, Andrew Flintoff and me, promenading down the street, waggling our behinds. He is younger than me, Andrew Flintoff, but he already has a wife and kiddies. Wifey must have uneasy dreams when he goes off on tour, dreams about hubby succumbing to the lures of someone like me, racy, exciting, exotic.

Similarly, in Vietnam, the readiness of Vietnamese insurgents to accept huge losses in frontal attacks on their American foes was attributed not to individual heroism but to Oriental fatalism. As for their commanders, their readiness to order such attacks proved their cynical disregard for the value of human life.

When the earliest of the suicide bombings took place in Israel, there may at first have been some moral ambivalence in the West. Blowing yourself up is, after all, more courageous ("takes more guts") than leaving a ticking bomb in a crowded place and walking away. But that ambivalence soon evaporated. Because suicide bombers sacrifice their lives for evil ends, the argument now went, they could never be true heroes. Furthermore, since they did not really value their lives (they believed that in the wink of an eye they would be translated to paradise), there was a sense in which they were not sacrificing anything at all.

We are not talking about life, she says. We are talking about typing. We are talking about spelling. Why does the English need to be spelled right anyway if it is going to be translated into German?

El Señor's eyesight isn't that good, according to him. Nevertheless, when I make my silky moves I can feel his eyes lock onto me. That is the game between him and me. I don't mind. What else is your bottom for? Use it or lose it.

When I am not carrying laundry baskets I am his segretaria, part-time. Also, now and again, his house-help. At first I was just supposed to be his segretaria, his secret aria, his scary fairy, in fact not even that, just his typist, his tipitista, his clackadackia.

Once upon a time there were wars (the Trojan War, for instance, or more recently the Anglo–Boer War) in which brave deeds on the part of one's foes were recognized, acknowledged, and remembered. That chapter in history seems to have closed. In today's wars there is no acceptance, even in principle, that the enemy can have heroes. Suicide bombers in the Israeli–Palestinian conflict or in occupied Iraq are looked upon in the West as lower than plain guerrilla fighters: whereas the guerrilla fighter may at least be said to offer some kind of martial contest, the suicide bomber fights – if he can be said to fight at all – dirty.

I shut my mouth. Criticism clearly peeves her. Never mind, I say, it will all become easier.

He dictates great thoughts into his machine, then hands over the tapes to me, plus a sheaf of papers in his half-blind scrawl, with the difficult words written out in careful block letters. I take away the tapes and listen to them on my earphones and solemnly type them out. Fix them up too here and there where I can, where they lack a certain something, a certain oomph, though he is supposed to be the big writer and I just the little Filipina.

One would like to retain some respect for any person who chooses death over dishonour, but in the case of Islamist suicide bombers respect does not come easily when one sees how many of them there are, and therefore (by a logical step that may be badly flawed, that may simply express the old Western prejudice against the mass mentality of the Other) how cheaply they must value life. In such a quandary, it may help to think of suicide bombings as a response, of a somewhat despairing nature, against American (and Israeli) achievements in guidance technology far beyond the capacities of their opponents. Defence contractors in the United States are at this moment working to bring into being a battlefield of the imperial future in which American personnel need no longer be physically present, in which death and destruction will be dealt out to the (human) enemy by robot soldiers guided electronically by technicians sitting in a battleship a hundred miles away or indeed in an operations room in the Pentagon. In the face of such an adversary, how can one save one's honour except by desperately and extravagantly throwing away one's life?

She pouts. I was expecting more of a story, she says. It is difficult to get into the swing when the subject keeps changing.

Segretaria. It sounds like a cocktail from Haiti: rum and pineapple juice and bull's-blood, shaken up with chipped ice and topped with a couple of rooster's testicles.

The truth is, he doesn't need a segretaria or even a tipista, he could type out his thoughts himself, they sell keyboards with super-size keys for people like him. But he doesn't like typing (has an "insuperable distaste," as he puts it), he prefers to squeeze the pen and feel the words come out at the other end. Nothing like the feel of words coming into the world, he says, it is enough to make you shiver. I draw myself up, make a prune mouth. You shouldn't say things like that to a nice girl, Señor, I say. And I turn my back and off I go with a waggle of the bum, his eyes avid upon me.

07. On Al Qaida

On television last night, a BBC documentary which argues that, for reasons of its own, the US administration chooses to keep alive the myth of Al Qaida as a powerful secret terrorist organization with cells all over the world, whereas the truth is that Al Qaida has been more or less destroyed and what we see today are terror attacks by autonomous groups of Muslim radicals.

I have no doubt that the main claims of the documentary are true: that "Islamic terrorism" is not a centrally controlled and directed conspiracy; and that the US administration is, perhaps deliberately, exaggerating the dangers faced by the public. If there were indeed a devilish organization with agents all over the world, bent on demoralizing Western populations and destroying Western civilization, it would surely by now have poisoned water supplies all over the place, or shot down commercial aircraft, or spread noxious germs – acts of terrorism that are easy enough to bring off.

Because it is too much to expect her to read my handwriting, I record each day's output on a dictaphone tape and give her both tape and manuscript to work from. It is a method I have used before, there is no reason why it should not work, though there is no denying my handwriting is deteriorating. I am losing motor control. That is part of my condition. That is part of what is happening to me. There are days when I squint at what I have just written, barely able to decipher it myself.

I picked it up from the ducks, I think: a shake of the tail so quick it is almost a shiver. Quick-quack. Why should we be too high and mighty to learn from ducks?

Where are you from? he demanded that first day in the laundry room where it all began. Why, from upstairs, kind sir, I said. I don't mean that, he said. Where were you born? Why do you want to know? I replied. Am I not blonde-eyed and blue-haired enough for your tastes?

Included in the television programme was the story of four young American Muslims on trial for planning an attack on Disneyland. During the trial the prosecution introduced a home video found in their apartment as evidence against them. The video was exceedingly amateurish. It included long footage of a garbage can and of the photographer's feet as he walked. The prosecution claimed that the amateurishness was feigned, that what we were witnessing was a reconnaissance tool: the garbage can was a potential hiding-place for a bomb, the walking feet paced out the distance from A to B.

The rationale offered by the prosecution for this paranoid interpretation was that the very amateurishness of the video was ground for suspicion, since, where Al Qaida is concerned, nothing is what it seems to be.

So we proceed in this error-strewn way. "Acquiring an italic identity." Who does she think I am – Aeneas? "Subject hood." The citizens of the state roaming the streets in their black hoods. Surreal images. Perhaps that is what she thinks it is to be a writer: you rave into a microphone, saying the first thing that comes into your head; then you hand over the mishmash to a girl, or to some aleatoric device, and wait to see what they will make of it.

By upstairs I didn't mean much, only that we have a unit twenty-five storeys up, twenty-five floors above him, with a sun-porch and a view of the harbour, if you squint. So he and I are neighbours of a kind, distant neighbours, El Señor and La Segretaria.

You shouldn't leave the blinds open after dark, I caution him, strangers will see what you get up to. What could I possibly get up to that would interest strangers? he says. I don't know, I say, people get up to surprising things. Well, he replies, they will soon get bored watching me, I am a human being no different from them. Nonsense, I say, we are all different, in subtle ways, we are not ants, we are not sheep. That is why we take a peek through the blinds when the blinds are left open: to see the subtle ways. It's only natural.

Where did the prosecutors learn to think in such a way? The answer: in literature classes in the United States of the 1980s and 1990s, where they were taught that in criticism suspiciousness is the chief virtue, that the critic must accept nothing whatsoever at face value. From their exposure to literary theory these not-very-bright graduates of the academy of the humanities in its postmodernist phase bore away a set of analytical instruments which they obscurely sensed could be useful outside the classroom, and an intuition that the ability to argue that nothing is as it seems to be might get you places. Putting those instruments in their hands was the *trahison des clercs* of our time. "You taught me language, and my profit on it is I know how to curse."

I inquire as casually as I can what kind of work she has done, what "hospitality" and "human resources" actually mean. Is that your way of asking if I have a diploma in typing? she replies. I couldn't care less about diplomas, I say, I am just trying to fill in the picture. I have done all kinds of things, she replies, this, that and the other, I haven't kept a list. But what does this, that and the other mean? I persist. OK, she replies, how about this: in June and July I worked as a receptionist. Temporarily. In a cathouse. I stare at her. A cathouse, she repeats with a straight face: you know, a home for cats.

Kurosawa. *The Seven Samurai.* How John Howard and the Liberals are just the seven samurai all over again. Who is going to believe that? I remember seeing *The Seven Samurai* in Taiwan, in Japanese with Chinese subtitles. Most of the time I didn't know what was going on. The only image that has stayed with me is of the long naked thighs of the crazy man with the topknot. Armour-plated shins, naked thighs, bare bottom: what fashions they had in those days! Enough to drive a girl wild.

08. On universities

It was always a bit of a lie that universities were self-governing institutions. Nevertheless, what universities suffered during the 1980s and 1990s was pretty shameful, as under threat of having their funding cut they allowed themselves to be turned into business enterprises, in which professors who had previously carried on their enquiries in sovereign freedom were transformed into harried employees required to fulfil quotas under the scrutiny of professional managers. Whether the old powers of the professoriat will ever be restored is much to be doubted.

A cathouse. I can see her at the front desk of a cathouse. Take a seat, make yourself comfortable, Ursula will be out in a minute, or would you prefer to see Tiffany?

And before the home for cats? I persevere.

Write about cricket, I suggest. Write your memoirs. Anything but politics. The kind of writing you do doesn't work with politics. Politics is about shouting other people down and getting your own way, not about logic. Write about the world around you. Write about the birds. There are always a mob of magpies strutting around the park as if they own it, he could write about them. Shoo, you monsters! I say, but of course they pay no heed. No brow, the skull running straight into the beak, no space for a brain.

What he says about politics sends me to sleep. Politics is all around us, it's like the air, it's like pollution. You can't fight pollution. Best to ignore it, or just get used to it, adapt.

In the days when Poland was under Communist rule, there were dissidents who conducted night classes in their homes, running seminars on writers and philosophers excluded from the official canon (for example, Plato). No money changed hands, though there may have been other forms of payment. If the spirit of the university is to survive, something along those lines may have to come into being in countries where tertiary education has been wholly subordinated to business principles. In other words, the real university may have to move into people's homes and grant degrees for which the sole backing will be the names of the scholars who sign the certificates.

If you wanted a CV you should have asked for it at the beginning, she says. Instead of hiring me on the basis of my looks. Do you want to call it quits right now? That would suit me. Then you can find someone else who meets your high standards. Or go to a bureau, like I suggested in the first place.

Alan comes into the room while I am typing. So what are you up to now? he says. Typing for the old man, I say. What is it about? he says. Samurai, I say. He comes and reads over my shoulder. Birth certificates for animals, he says – is he crazy? Does he want to give them all names? Clifford John Rat. Susan Annabel Rat. What about death certificates too, while he is about it? When are you coming to bed?

09. On Guantanamo Bay

Someone should put together a ballet under the title *Guantanamo, Guantanamo!* A corps of prisoners, their ankles shackled together, thick felt mittens on their hands, muffs over their ears, black hoods over their heads, do the dances of the persecuted and desperate. Around them, guards in olive-green uniforms prance with demonic energy and glee, cattle prods and billy-clubs at the ready. They touch the prisoners with the prods and the prisoners leap; they wrestle prisoners to the ground and shove the clubs up their anuses and the prisoners go into spasms. In a corner, a man on stilts in a Donald Rumsfeld mask alternately writes at his lectern and dances ecstatic little jigs.

One day it will be done, though not by me. It may even be a hit in London and Berlin and New York. It will have absolutely no effect on the people it targets, who could not care less what ballet audiences think of them.

Please, I say. Please don't take it amiss.

Don't take what amiss? Being told that I can't type?

Of course you can type. I know this job is beneath you, I am sorry about that, but let us just persevere, let us just go on.

Three years together and still Alan has the hots for me, hots so hot there are times I think he is going to burst. He likes me to talk about my exes while he is at it. And then? he says. And then? And then? Then he made me take him in my mouth, I say. This mouth? he says. These lips? And gives me mad, furious kisses. Yes, these lips, I say, tearing myself loose from his kisses long enough to speak, and he bursts.

All lies, of course. I make them up to inflame him. That stuff you told me, he says afterwards – it is all lies, isn't it? All lies, I say, and give him a mystery smile. Always keep a man guessing.

10. On national shame

An article in a recent *New Yorker* makes it as plain as day that the US administration, with the lead taken by Richard Cheney, not only sanctions the torture of prisoners taken in the so-called war on terror but is active in every way to subvert laws and conventions proscribing torture. We may thus legitimately speak of an administration which, while legal in the sense of being legally elected, is illegal or anti-legal in the sense of operating beyond the bounds of the law, evading the law, and resisting the rule of law.

Their shamelessness is quite extraordinary. Their denials are less than half-hearted. The distinction their hired lawyers draw between torture and coercion is patently insincere, *pro forma*. In the new dispensation we have created, they implicitly say, the old powers of shame have been abolished. Whatever abhorrence you may feel counts for nothing. You cannot touch us, we are too powerful.

Demosthenes: Whereas the slave fears only pain, what the free man fears most is shame. If we grant the truth of what the *New Yorker* claims, then the issue for individual Americans becomes a moral one: how, in the face of this shame to which I am subjected, do I behave? How do I save my honour?

Thus I do my best to mollify her. *Thank God I am not Mr Aberdeen,* I think, *married to this tetchy young woman.* But that is nonsense, of course. I would give my right hand to be Mr Aberdeen.

*

What about the old man, he says – he hasn't tried anything with you, has he? Has he given me a poke, do you mean? I say. No, he hasn't given me a poke. Hasn't tried. But what if he had? What would you do? Go downstairs and bash him? You will land up in the papers that way. Make a laughing-stock of yourself. Well-known writer biffed by jealous lover.

Suicide would save one's honour, and perhaps there have already been honour suicides among Americans that one does not hear of. But what of political action? Will political action – not armed resistance but action within the ground rules of the democratic system (circulating petitions, organizing meetings, writing letters) – suffice?

Dishonour is no respecter of fine distinctions. Dishonour descends upon one's shoulders, and once it has descended no amount of clever pleading will dispel it. In the present climate of whipped-up fear, and in the absence of any groundswell of popular revulsion against torture, political actions by individual citizens seem unlikely to have any practical effect. Yet perhaps, pursued doggedly and in a spirit of outrage, such actions will at least allow people to hold their heads up. Mere symbolic actions, on the other hand – burning the flag, pronouncing aloud the words "I abhor the leaders of my country and dissociate myself from them" – will certainly not be enough.

Impossible to believe that in some American hearts the spectacle of their country's honour being dragged through the mud does not breed murderous thoughts. Impossible to believe that no one has yet plotted to assassinate these criminals in high office.

Do you think I could do modelling? she says, out of the blue.

She is in my flat. She has just dropped off the day's typing; she is on her way out, but for some reason chooses to linger. She puts her hands on her hips, tosses her hair, glances at me provocatively.

He hasn't tried anything while I am with him, but what he gets up to after I exit is another story. God alone witnesses what he gets up to then, God and the blessed virgin and the chorus of saints. There is a pair of panties of mine he pinched from the dryer, I am sure of it. My guess is he unbuttons himself when I am gone and wraps himself in my undies and closes his eyes and summons up visions of my divine behind and makes himself come. And then buttons up and gets back to John Howard and George Bush, what villains they are.

Has there perhaps already been a Stauffenberg plot, record of which will at some time in the future emerge into the light of day?

In any event, without much prospect of a reversal of policy, the object, not just for Americans of conscience but for individual Westerners in general, must be to find ways to save one's honour, which is to a degree the same as keeping one's self-respect but is also a matter of not having to appear with soiled hands before the judgment of history.

The judgment of history is clearly a matter that exercises the minds of the US administration too. History will judge us on the basis of the record we leave behind, they say in public; and over that record, they remind themselves in private, we have an unparalleled degree of control. Of the worst of our crimes let no trace survive, textual or physical. Let the files be shredded, the hard drives smashed, the bodies burned, the ashes scattered.

Of Richard Nixon they are scornful. Nixon was an amateur, they say. Nixon was casual about security. On their priority list, security – by which they mean secrecy – comes first, second, and third.

Modelling, I say; they generally go for taller girls in modelling. Taller and younger. You would find yourself in competition with skinny sixteen-year-olds.

That is what I meant about leaving the blinds open and giving people a shock.

Alan votes Howard. As for me, I thought I wouldn't, in the 2004 election, but then at the last minute I did. Better the devil you know than the devil you don't, I said to myself. They tell you you have three years to make up your mind, from one election to the next, but that isn't true. You always wait till the last second to make up your mind. It is like with Alan, when he put the question. Shall we? he said. I needn't have answered yes, I could have answered no. But I didn't. And now here we are living together, Mr Haystack and Ms Needle, tight as twins.

The worst of their deeds we will never know: that we must be prepared to accept. To know the worst, we will have to extrapolate and use the imagination. The worst is likely to be whatever we think them capable of (capable of ordering, capable of turning a blind eye to); and what they are capable of is, all too plainly, anything.

There is as yet no evidence that Australians have participated in actual atrocities. Either the Americans have not put pressure on them to join in, or there has been pressure and they have resisted. One Australian intelligence officer, a man named Rod Barton, a scientific specialist who found himself participating in the interrogation of Iraqi scientists, broke ranks, made his story public, and then, to his great credit, resigned from the service.

The Australian government, on the other hand, has been the most abject of the so-called Coalition of the Willing, and has even been prepared to suffer with no more than a tight little smile the humiliation of getting nothing in return. In negotiations with the United States on terms of bilateral trade, its pleas for concessions, in view of its faithful collaboration in Iraq and elsewhere, have received short shrift. It has been dutifully silent on the subject of David Hicks, the young Australian Muslim imprisoned by the Americans in Guantanamo Bay. Indeed, his plight has evoked in certain cabinet ministers a vengefulness, a moral meanness, worthy of Donald Rumsfeld or of the younger Bush himself.

I wasn't talking about that kind of modelling, she says. What kind of modelling then? I say. Photographic modelling, she says.

Shall we or shan't we? said Alan that night at Ronaldo's. Shall I or shan't I? I said to myself. Eeny-meeny-miny-mo. That is how Howard got elected. The nigger you catch by the toe. The nigger you know. Oops. Negro.

As I said, his eyesight is shot, El Señor's. "My eyesight is going, and everything else too, but principally my eyesight." That is why he talks about squeezing worms out of his pen. The pages of writing he hands over are no use to me, no practical use. He forms his letters clearly enough, m's and n's and u's and w's included, but when he has to write a whole passage he can't keep

Yet although it has been complicit in America's crimes, to say that Australia has fallen into the same anti-legality or extra-legality as America has would be stretching a point. This state of affairs may soon change. In the new powers of policing that the Australian government is in the process of awarding itself, one detects a comparable contempt for the rule of law. These are extraordinary times, runs the mantra, and extraordinary times demand extraordinary measures. It may not take much of a push for Australia to slide into the same condition as America, where on the basis of denunciations from informers ("sources") people simply vanish or are vanished from society, and publicizing their disappearance qualifies as a crime in its own right.

Is dishonour a state of being that comes in shades and degrees? If there is a state of deep dishonour, is there a state of mild dishonour too, dishonour lite? The temptation is to say no: if one is in dishonour one is in dishonour. Yet if today I heard that some American had committed suicide rather than live in disgrace, I would fully understand; whereas an Australian who committed suicide in response to the actions of the Howard government would risk seeming comical.

She makes a moue, wriggles her hips. You know, she says. Wouldn't you like a picture of me? You could put it on your desk.

the line straight, it dips like a plane nosediving into the sea or a baritone running out of breath. Never up, always down.

Bad eyes, teeth even worse. If I was him I would have the lot pulled out and get a nice new pair of dentures fitted. No wife would put up with teeth like that, she would send him off to the dentist one-two-three, click-clack-clack. Get those teeth of yours fixed or I am leaving. He was married once. I know because I asked him. So, Señor C, I said, have you never been married? Yes, I have been married, he replied. I waited for more: how many children, when his wife died if she died, what she died of, that sort of thing.

The American administration has raised vengefulness to an infernal level, whereas the meanness of the Australians is as yet merely petty.

The generation of white South Africans to which I belong, and the next generation, and perhaps the generation after that too, will go bowed under the shame of the crimes that were committed in their name. Those among them who endeavour to salvage personal pride by pointedly refusing to bow before the judgment of the world suffer from a burning resentment, a bristling anger at being condemned without adequate hearing, that in psychic terms may turn out to be an equally heavy burden. Such people might learn a trick or two from the British about managing collective guilt. The British have simply declared their independence from their imperial forebears. The Empire was long ago abolished, they say, so what is there for us to feel responsible for? And anyway, the people who ran the Empire were Victorians, dour, stiff folk in dark clothes, nothing like us.

Is yesterday's quarrel forgotten – forgiven and forgotten? Perhaps. Or perhaps she does not remember it as a quarrel. Perhaps it flitted over her consciousness like the merest breath of wind across water.

But that was all: *Yes, I have been married,* as if I was to understand, *Yes, I have been married and I didn't like it and don't want to talk about it.*

Alan used to be married, I volunteered. Did I tell you that? He left his wife to be with me. Cost him a lot of money.

I have to volunteer because he never asks anything, not after he asked about my background. *Where are you from?* he asked that first day, and I answered, *Why, from upstairs, kind sir.* He didn't

A few days ago I heard a performance of the Sibelius fifth symphony. As the closing bars approached, I experienced exactly the large, swelling emotion that the music was written to elicit. What would it have been like, I wondered, to be a Finn in the audience at the first performance of the symphony in Helsinki nearly a century ago, and feel that swell overtake one? The answer: one would have felt proud, proud that *one of us* could put together such sounds, proud that out of nothing we human beings can make such stuff. Contrast with that one's feelings of shame that *we, our people,* have made Guantanamo. Musical creation on the one hand, a machine for inflicting pain and humiliation on the other: the best and the worst that human beings are capable of.

Since every word she says is charming, she is free to say whatever comes into her head. Similarly, since everything she does must be cute, she is free to do whatever she feels like. A spoiled child's way of thinking. The trouble is, she is not a child any more. It leaves a disturbing taste.

*

---

like that. Too cheeky. Lots of empty bottles in his kitchen, which I am not supposed to notice. Cockroaches too. Shows how long ago the wife must have died or run away. Scurry-scurry along the skirting boards when they think you aren't looking. Crumbs everywhere, even on his desk. Cockroach heaven. No wonder his teeth are so bad. Crunch-crunch scribble-scribble talk-talk. Down with the Liberals. What Hobbes said. What Machiavelli said. Ho hum.

II. On the curse

In a book on ancient Greek religion, an essay by a man named Versnel from Leiden about certain inscribed lead tablets recovered from temples in the ancient world. Since these tablets typically invoke the aid of a god to put right some wrong done to a petitioner, Versnel calls them "curse tablets."

From Memphis, fourth century BCE, a curse tablet (in Greek) left at the temple of Oserapis: "O Lord Oserapis and you gods who sit enthroned together with Oserapis, to you I direct a prayer, I, Artemisia . . . against the father of my daughter, who robbed her of her death gifts (?) and of her coffin . . . Exactly in the way that he did injustice to me and to my children, in that way Oserapis and the gods should bring it about that he be not buried by his children and that he himself not be able to bury his parents. As long as my accusation against him lies here, may he perish miserably, on land or sea . . ." [4]

I ask her about Alan, about what he does. Alan is an investment consultant, she says. Is he independent? I ask. He is in a partnership, she says, but he is pretty independent, all the partners are pretty independent, it is that kind of partnership. Might Alan be prepared to offer me advice on investments? I inquire.

Usually they keep a picture of the spouse in the bedroom, in the bloom of his/her youth. Or a wedding photograph, the happy couple. And then the children one after the other in a row. But in his bedroom, nothing. On the wall a framed scroll in some foreign language (Latin?) with his name in fancy lettering with lots of curlicues and a big red wax seal in the corner. His credentials? His diploma? The licence that allows him to practise? I didn't know you needed a licence to practise as a writer. I thought it was just something you did if you had the knack.

Mrs Saunders says he is from Colombia, but it turns out she is wrong, he isn't from South America at all.

There must be people all over today's world who, refusing to accept that there is no justice in the universe, invoke the help of their gods against America, an America that has proclaimed itself beyond the reach of the law of nations. Even if the gods do not respond today or tomorrow, the petitioners tell themselves, they may yet be stirred to action a generation or two down the line. Their plea thus becomes in effect a curse: let the memory of the wrong that has been done to us not fade away, let punishment be visited on the wrongdoer in generations to come.

This is very much the deep theme of William Faulkner: the theft of the land from the Indians or the rape of slave women comes back in unforeseen form, generations later, to haunt the oppressor. Looking back, the inheritor of the curse shakes his head ruefully.

She hesitates. I will ask him, she says; but normally he doesn't like to work with friends. I am not a friend, I say, just someone who happens to live downstairs; but never mind, I was just curious. How long has Alan been in this partnership?

Seven years. He was one of the founding partners.

I never undertook, when I accepted the job, to cart away the bottles and fix up the bathroom and spray the roaches. But you can't let a man live in such filth. It is an insult. An insult to whom? To visitors. To the parents that brought him into the world. To common decency.

Alan wants to know how much money he has. How should I know, I say, he doesn't talk to me about finances. Look in his drawers, says Alan. Look in the kitchen cupboards. Look for a shoebox: that is the giveaway, he is the kind to keep his money in a shoebox. Tied with a string? I say. A string or a rubber band, says Alan. Alan never knows when I am making fun of him. Such a doof. What do I do when I find the shoebox? I say. Take the money, put back the box where you found it, he says. And then? I say – And then, when he calls the police? OK, wait till they cart him off to the morgue, then take the money, says Alan, the box

We thought they were powerless, he says, *that was why we did what we did; now we see they were not powerless at all.*

"Tragic guilt," writes Jean-Pierre Vernant, "takes shape in the constant clash between the ancient religious conception of the misdeed as a defilement attached to an entire race and inexorably transmitted from one generation to the next . . . , and the new concept adopted in law according to which the guilty one is defined as a private individual who, acting under no constraint, has deliberately chosen to commit a crime."[5]

The drama being played out before our eyes is of a ruler, George W. Bush (whether Bush turns out to have been a pawn in the hands of others is not relevant here), whose hubris lies in denying the force of the curse on him and of curses in general; who indeed goes further and asserts that he cannot commit a crime, since he is the one who makes the laws defining crimes.

And how long have you and he been married?

We are not married. I thought I told you that. We don't make a big thing about it. I mean, whatever people assume – we are married, we are not married – we just let it slide.

---

and the money, before the vultures arrive. What vultures? I say. The relatives, says Alan.

Alan has got it all wrong, but I check the cupboards anyway, just to make sure – the bathroom cupboards, the kitchen cupboards, all the drawers in the bedroom. In a solitary shoebox, a shoe-cleaning kit: brushes with the bristles falling out, shoe polish that caked years ago.

He must have a safe, says Alan. Look behind the pictures on the wall. Or else it is in the bank, I say, where normal people keep their money. He is not normal, says Alan. Of course he is not normal, not supernaturally normal, I say, but how normal do you need to be to keep your money in a bank? And what entitles us to steal his money anyway? It is not stealing, says Alan, not if he is dead. Anyway, if we don't take it someone else will. It is not stealing if he is dead? I say. That's news to me. Don't be irritating, you know what I mean, says Alan.

49

In the outrages he and his servants perform, notably the outrage of torture, and in his hubristic claim to be above the law, the younger Bush challenges the gods, and by the very shamelessness of that challenge ensures that the gods will visit punishment upon the children and grandchildren of his house.

The case is not unique, even in our times. Young Germans protest, *We have no blood on our hands, so why are we looked on as racists and murderers?* The answer: *Because you have the misfortune to be the grandchildren of your grandparents; because you carry a curse.*

So you have no plans for children.

On the contrary, I don't have the faintest idea what Alan means. Why this obsession of his with the old man and his money? It is not as though he doesn't rake in pots of money of his own. But something in the whole picture offends him, as though the old man were a Spanish galleon going down on the high seas with a hold full of gold from the Indies, that would be lost for ever if he, Alan, didn't dive in and save it.

Alan looked him up on the internet. That is how I found out he isn't from Colombia, isn't a Señor at all. Born South Africa 1934, it said. Novelist and critic. Long list of titles and dates. Nothing about a wife. Bella Saunders swears he is from South America, I said. Are you sure you have got the right man? Alan brought up a picture on the screen. Isn't that him? And indeed it

The curse comes into being at the moment when the man of power pauses and says to himself, *People say that, if I commit this act, I and my house will be cursed — shall I go ahead?* And then answers himself, *Pah! there are no gods, there is no such thing as a curse!*

The impious one brings down a curse upon his descendants; in return, his descendants curse his name.

No. Alan doesn't want children.

---

was, though the picture must have been taken years ago, when he was not bad-looking, as men go, instead of just skull and bones.

Can I make a criticism? I said yesterday, when I brought him his typing. Your English is very good, considering, but we don't say talk radio, that doesn't make sense, we say talkback radio.

Considering? he said. Considering what?

Considering it isn't your mother tongue.

Mother tongue, he said. What does that mean, mother tongue?

It means the tongue you learned at your mother's knee, I said.

I know that, he said. It is your choice of metaphor that I am querying. Do I have to have learned language at a woman's knee? Do I have to have drunk it from a woman's breast?

12. On paedophilia

The current hysteria about sexual acts with children – not only such acts in themselves but fictive representations of them in the form of so-called "child pornography" – gives rise to some strange illogicalities. When Stanley Kubrick filmed *Lolita* thirty years ago, he got around the taboo – relatively mild in those days – by using an actress who was well known not to be a child and could only with difficulty be disguised as one. But in today's climate that stratagem would not work: the fact (the ficto-fact, the idea) that the fictional character is a child would trump the fact that the image on the screen is not that of a child. When the issue is sex with minors, the law, with public opinion baying behind it, is simply not in the mood for fine distinctions.

There is an innocent, a purely sociable, an even routine way of raising the question of children. At the moment when I pronounce the first word, the word *So*, my curiosity could not be more innocent. But in between *So* and the second word *you* the devil waylays me, sends me an image of this Anya on a sweaty summer night, convulsed in the arms of ginger-haired, freckle-shouldered Alan, opening her womb in gladness to the gush of his male juices.

I am rebuked, I said. Please accept humble apologies from this unworthy person.

He gave me a hard stare. Where do I say talk radio? he said.

I pointed to the place. He peered, peered again, crossed out the word *talk*, and in the margin, in pencil, painstakingly wrote *talkback*. There, he said, is that better?

Much better, I said. Your eyesight isn't that bad.

Most of the time he wears a mustard-coloured tweed jacket that could come from a 1950s British movie and gives off a bad smell, like old lemon rinds. When he asks me to read over his shoulder I find some excuse not to. I ought to sneak into his flat during the night and steal the jacket and have it drycleaned. Or burn it.

How on earth did the present climate develop? Until the feminists entered the fray at the latter end of the twentieth century, morally minded censors had been suffering one defeat after another and were everywhere on the defensive. But on the issue of pornography, feminism, in other respects a progressive movement, chose to go to bed with the religious conservatives, and all became confusion. Thus today, while on the one hand the public media with impunity lead the way into grosser and grosser sexual display, on the other hand the aestheticist argument that art trumps taboo (art "transforms" its material, purging it of its ugliness), and therefore that the artist should be above the law, has been given a thorough battering. In a few well-defined areas taboo has emerged triumphant: not only are certain representations, notably of sex with minors, proscribed and ferociously punished, but discussion of the basis of the taboo is frowned on too, if not barred.

By the time the monosyllable *you* has been fully enounced she can see, by a kind of magical transference or perhaps simply from the image on my retina, what I am seeing. If blushing were in her repertoire, she would blush. But it is not. Do you mean, she says coolly, are we using birth control? And she gives the tiniest little smile, as if to beckon me on. Yes, she says, answering her own question, we are using birth control. Of a kind.

This stuff I am typing – how much of it will there be? I said.

The stuff you are typing, he replied, insofar as it is a set of opinions, day-by-day opinions, counts as a miscellany. A miscellany is not like a novel, with a beginning and a middle and an end. I don't know how long it will be. As long as the Germans want it to be.

Why do you write this stuff? Why don't you write another novel instead? Isn't that what you are good at, novels?

A novel? No. I don't have the endurance any more. To write a novel you have to be like Atlas, holding up a whole world on your shoulders and supporting it there for months and years while its affairs work themselves out. It is too much for me as I am today.

The radical feminist attack on pornography, led by such people as Catharine MacKinnon, had two prongs. First, images of adult males having sex with children (that is to say, either with children playing children or with actors of whatever age playing children) were claimed to encourage real-world violations of real-world children. Second, inducing children or indeed women to perform sexual acts before the camera was claimed to be a form of sexual exploitation (in the pornography industry as it exists today, ran the argument, women operate under inherent duress).

Some piquant hypothetical questions suggest themselves. Should there be a ban upon publishing in print form a story, a self-proclaimed fiction, in which an appropriately petite twenty-year-old actress plays for the camera the role of a child having sex with an adult man? If not, why insist upon a ban on a filmed version of the same story, which is no more than a transposition from conventional (verbal) to natural (photographic) signs?

Now dare to ask me, her eyes say – *dare to ask me what kind of birth control.*

Of a kind, I say. Mm . . . I won't ask of what kind. But let me offer you a word of benevolent advice: don't leave it too late.

Still, I said, we have all got opinions, especially about politics. If you tell a story at least people will shut up and listen to you. A story or a joke.

Stories tell themselves, they don't get told, he said. That much I know after a lifetime of working with stories. Never try to impose yourself. Wait for the story to speak for itself. Wait and hope that it isn't born deaf and dumb and blind. I could do that when I was younger. I could wait patiently for months on end. Nowadays I get tired. My attention wanders.

And me, I said – am I going to wind up among your opinions too? Do you have opinions you plan to share with the world about secretaries?

What of the representation of children having sex not with adults but with other children? The new orthodoxy would seem to be that what renders the image culpable is not the idea of sex between minors (many of whom lead active and even indiscriminate sex lives) nor the fact of sex, real or simulated, between actors who are minors, but the presence of an adult eye somewhere in the scene, either behind the camera or in the darkened auditorium. Whether a film made by minors using minor actors engaging in sexual acts and displayed only to minors would infringe the taboo is an interesting question. Presumably not. Yet not long ago, in one of the American states, a seventeen-year-old boy was sent to jail for having sex with his fifteen-year-old girlfriend (he was denounced to the law by her parents).

You sound like you speak from experience, she says. Did you never have children of your own?

He gave me a sharp look.
Because if you are going to use me, remember, you owe me an appearance fee.

As for sex between teachers and students, so strong is the tide of disapproval nowadays that uttering even the mildest word in its defence becomes (exactly) like battling that tide, feeling your puny stroke quite overwhelmed by a great heft of water bearing you backward. What you face when you open your lips to speak is not the silencing stroke of the censor but an edict of exile.

No, I didn't, I say. Children are a gift from above. It appears I did not merit the gift.

I'm sorry to hear that, she says.

*

I thought it a pretty smart remark, for a mere Segretaria.
I repeated it to Alan afterwards. If he uses you in his book, you can sue, said Alan at once. Alan never misses a chance. Sharp as a knife. Sue him and his publishers too. Sue for *crimen injuria*. It would make a huge stink in the papers. Then we could settle out of court.

13. On the body

We speak of *the dog with the sore foot* or *the bird with the broken wing*. But the dog does not think of itself in those terms, or the bird. To the dog, when it tries to walk, there is simply *I am pain*, to the bird, when it launches itself into flight, simply *I cannot*.

With us it seems to be different. The fact that such common locutions as "my leg," "my eye," "my brain," and even "my body" exist suggests that we believe there is some non-material, perhaps fictive, entity that stands in the relation of possessor to possessed to the body's "parts" and even to the whole body. Or else the existence of such locutions shows that language cannot get purchase, cannot get going, until it has split up the unity of experience.

Last night I had a bad dream, which I afterwards wrote down, about dying and being guided to the gateway to oblivion by a young woman. What I did not record is the question that occurred to me in the act of writing: *Is she the one?*

Why would I want to sue him?

Wake up. He can't just do what he likes with you. He can't pick on you and have obscene fantasies about you and then sell them to the public for profit. Also, he can't take down your words and publish them without your permission. That is plagiarism. It is worse than plagiarism. You have an identity, which belongs to you alone. It is your most valuable possession, from a certain point of view, which you are entitled to protect. Vigorously.

All parts of the body are not cathected to the same degree. If a tumour were cut out of my body and displayed to me on a surgical tray as "your tumour," I would feel revulsion at an object that is in a sense "of" me but that I disown, and indeed rejoice at the elimination of; whereas if one of my hands were cut off and displayed to me, I would no doubt feel the keenest grief.

About hair, fingernail clippings, and so forth one has no feelings, since their loss belongs to a cycle of renewal.

Teeth are more mysterious. The teeth in "my" mouth are "my" teeth, part of "me," but my feeling for them is less intimate than my feeling for, say, my lips. They feel neither more nor less "mine" than the metal or porcelain prostheses in my mouth, the handiwork of dentists whose very names I have forgotten. I feel myself to be owner or custodian of my teeth rather than feeling my teeth to be part of me. If a rotten tooth were to be extracted and displayed to me, I would feel no great sorrow, even though my body ("I") will never regenerate it.

These thoughts about the body occur not in the abstract but in

---

This young woman who declines to call me by my name, instead calling me *Señor* or perhaps *Senior* – is she the one who has been assigned to conduct me to my death? If that is so, how odd a

---

Don't be silly, Alan. He is not going to give me his fantasies to type if it is me he is having fantasies about.

Why not? Maybe that is how he gets his kicks: making the woman read his fantasies about her. It is logical, in a back-to-front way. It is a means of exercising power over a woman when you can't fuck any more.

relation to a specific person, X, unnamed. On the morning of the day he died, X brushed his teeth, taking care of them with the due diligence we learn as children. From his ablutions he emerged to face the day, and before the day had ended he was dead. His spirit departed, leaving behind a body that was good for nothing, worse than good for nothing because it would soon begin to decay and become a threat to public health. Part of that dead body was the full set of teeth he had brushed that morning, teeth that had also died in the sense that blood had ceased to course through their roots, yet that paradoxically ceased to suffer decay as the body cooled and its oral bacteria cooled too, and were extinguished.

If X had been buried in the earth, the parts of "his" body that had lived most intensely, that were most "he," would have rotted away, while "his" teeth, which he might have felt to have merely been in his care and custody, would have survived long into the future. But of course X was not buried but cremated; and the people who built the oven in which he was consumed ensured that it was hot enough to turn everything to ash, even bones, even teeth. Even teeth.

---

messenger, and how unsuitable! Yet perhaps it is the nature of death that everything about it, every last thing, should strike us as unsuitable.

Come on, Alan! You want me to dress up in convent-school uniform and appear in court as some virginal type who blushes when a man has thoughts about her? I will be thirty in March. Lots of men have had thoughts about me.

14. On the slaughter of animals

To most of us, what we see when we watch cooking programmes on television looks perfectly normal: kitchen utensils on the one hand, items of raw food on the other, on their way to being transformed into cooked food. But to someone unused to eating meat, the spectacle must be highly unnatural. For among the fruit and vegetables and oils and herbs and spices lie chunks of flesh hacked mere days ago from the body of some creature killed purposely and with violence. Animal flesh looks much the same as human flesh (why should it not?). So, to the eye unused to carnivore cuisine, the inference does not come automatically ("naturally") that the flesh on display is cut from a carcass (animal) rather than from a corpse (human).

It is important that not everyone should lose this way of seeing the kitchen – seeing it with what Viktor Shklovsky would call an estranged eye, as a place where, after the murders, the bodies of the dead are brought to be done up (disguised) before they are devoured (we rarely eat flesh raw; indeed, raw flesh is dangerous to our health).

A spectre from the past. By the roadside outside Nowra, half hidden in the grass, the body of a fox, a vixen, her eyes pecked out, her fur dulled, flattened by the night's rain. *How unsuitable*, that neat little fox would say.

It has nothing to do with age. Why, we would say to the court, would he pay three times the going rate for a typist? Answer: because what he is writing about you is humiliating, and the point of the exercise is to make you accept and endorse your own humiliation. Which is true, basically. He invites you to his flat to listen to filthy talk, then he has fantasies about doing things to you, then when you have listened to his fantasies on tape and copied them out word for word he pays you like he would pay a whore. It is worse than *crimen injuria*. It is abuse, psychological and sexual abuse. We could nail him for it.

On national television a few nights ago, amid the cooking programmes, a documentary was broadcast about what goes on in the abattoir in Port Said where cattle exported to Egypt from Australia meet their end. A reporter with a camera hidden in his backpack filmed scenes of cattle having their hind tendons slashed in order to make controlling them easier; in addition he claimed to have footage, too gruesome to broadcast, of a beast being stabbed in the eye, and the knife embedded in the eye socket then being used to twist the head to present the throat to the butcher's knife.

The veterinary supervisor of the slaughterhouse was interviewed. Unaware of the secret filming, he denied that anything untoward ever took place there. His slaughterhouse was a model establishment, he said.

Atrocities at the Port Said facility, and in the live export trade in general, have for a while been a source of concern to Australians. Cattle exporters have even donated to the slaughterhouse a killing-bed, a huge mechanism that traps the animal between bars and then lifts and rotates it bodily to make the death-stroke easier.

If I had been told that the last of my infatuations would be with a girl with provocative manners and cathouse connections (*a cathouse – you know, a home for cats*), I would have supposed I was destined to suffer one of those derided deaths in which the patron of the house of ill repute has a heart attack *in medias res* and his corpse has to be hastily dressed and smuggled out and

---

You are crazy, Alan. I am not in his book. It is about politics. It is about John Howard and George Bush. It is about samurai with bare bums. There is no sex.

How do you know? Maybe the sex is in passages he hides away from you. Maybe you are in tomorrow's instalment. You can't be sure. Why do you think he chose you when he could have got in a professional typist, some old battleaxe with sensible shoes and warts on her chin? Did he ask to see a specimen of your work? No. Did he ask for references? No. Did he ask you to show him your tits? I don't know. Maybe he did, and you aren't telling me.

The killing-bed stands unused. The slaughterers found it too much trouble, said the veterinarian.

It is too much to expect that a single fifteen-minute television programme should have a lasting effect on the conduct of the cattle trade. It would be ludicrous to expect hardened Egyptian abattoir workers to single out cattle from Australia for special, gentler treatment during their last hour on earth. And indeed common sense is on the workers' side. If an animal is going to have its throat cut, does it really matter that it has its leg tendons cut too? The notion of compassionate killing is riddled with absurdities. What well-meaning welfare campaigners seem to desire is that the beast should arrive before its executioner in a calm state of mind, and that death should overtake it before it realizes what is going on. But how can an animal be in a calm state of mind after being goaded off a ship onto the back of a truck and driven through teeming streets to a strange place reeking of blood and death? The animal is confused and desperate and no doubt difficult to control. That is why it has its tendons hacked.

---

dumped in an alley. But no, if the new dream is to be trusted it will not be like that. I will expire in my own bed and be discovered by my typist, who will close my eyes and pick up the telephone to make her report.

*

He chose you and no one else because he letches after you, Anya. Because he has lewd dreams where you suck his filthy old withered dick and then lash him afterwards with a cat-of-nine-tails. And what does that add up to? False advertising. Soliciting. Sexual harassment. We are going to nail him!

By now I was laughing. I love that crazy energy in Alan. Good or bad, people like him make the world go round. Come to me, mister, I said, come show me some real sexual harassment. And we sank down onto the bed. Curtain.

*

15. On avian influenza

It would appear that certain viruses, most notably the virus that causes avian influenza, are able to migrate from the species that normally host them to human beings. The 1918 influenza pandemic would seem to have been the work of an avian virus.

If we can speak meaningfully of viruses as possessing or being possessed by a drive or instinct, it is an instinct to replicate and multiply. As they multiply they take over more and more host organisms. It can hardly be their intention (so to speak) to kill their hosts. What they would like, rather, is an ever-expanding population of hosts. Ultimately what a virus wants is to take over the world, that is to say, to take up residence in every warm-blooded body. The death of any individual host is therefore a form of collateral damage, a mistake or miscalculation.

What I did not appreciate when I offered Anya the job was that, her days being more or less empty, work is for her a positive relief from tedium. Her days are empty because she is doing nothing to find employment, in hospitality or human resources or anywhere else. As for Mr A, it would seem to be enough that he wake up in the mornings with his girl beside him in bed, and that the same girl be at the door to welcome him home in the evenings with a drink in her hand.

If you really don't know what to write about, I said to Señor C, why not write reminiscences of your love life? That is what people like best – gossip, sex, romance, all the juicy details. You must have known lots of women in your day.

That made him perk up. Men like to be told they have a scandalous past.

Would that I could follow your advice, my dear Anya, he said. But, alas, it is a collection of opinions I am committed to, not a memoir. A response to the present in which I find myself.

The method used by the virus to cross from one species to another, the method of random mutation – try everything, see what works – cannot be said to be arrived at by rational planning. The individual virus does not have a brain and therefore *a fortiori* does not have a mind. But if we want to be resolutely materialist, we can say that the thinking (the rational thinking) employed by human beings as they try to find ways of annihilating the virus or denying it a home in the human population is also a process of trying out biochemical, neurological options, under the command of some master neurological programme called the reasoning process, and seeing which one works. To a radical materialist, the broad picture is thus of two forms of life each thinking about the other in its own way – human beings thinking about viral threats in the human way and viruses thinking about prospective hosts in a viral way.

What Anya mainly does to fill the dead hours is shop. At around eleven in the morning, three or four days a week, she will drop off the typing she has done. Come in, have a cup of coffee, I will suggest. She will shake her head. I have shopping to do, she will say. Really? What more can you possibly need to buy? I will ask. She will give a mysterious smile. Stuff, she will say.

Still, I said, you can always work the past in. It is not as if you don't have memories, sitting at your desk, letting your mind wander. Tell a few stories and you will come across as more human, more flesh and blood. You don't mind me giving my opinion, do you? Because a typist is not meant to be just a typing machine.

What is a typist meant to be then, he said, if not a typing machine?

It wasn't said in an aggressive way. It sounded like a real question, as if he genuinely wanted to know.

A typist is a human being, a man or a woman as the case may be, I said. In my case a woman. Or do you prefer not to think of me in that way?

68

The protagonists are involved in a strategic game, a game resembling chess in the sense that the one side attacks, creating pressure aimed at a breakthrough, while the other defends and searches for weak points at which to counterattack.

What is disturbing about the metaphor of relations between human beings and viruses as a chess game is that the virus always plays with the white pieces and we human beings with the black. The virus makes its move, and we react.

Two parties who embark on a game of chess implicitly agree to play by the rules. But in the game we play against the viruses there is no such founding convention. It is not inconceivable that one day a virus will make the equivalent of a conceptual leap and, instead of playing the game, will begin to play the game of game-playing, that is to say, will begin to reform the rules to suit its own desire.

By stuff she means clothes. I discovered this on my first visit to their penthouse, when without prompting she took me on a tour that included her dressing room. A long time since I last saw a dedicated dressing room. Racks and racks of stuff, enough to outfit a middle-sized cathouse. Don't you have a shoe collection too? I said.

Of course he thought of me in that way. He would have to be made of stone not to, what with the scent of me, and my tits in his face. Poor old guy! What could he say? What could he do? Helpless as a babe. *What are you if you are not a typing machine?* What a question! *What about you? What kind of machine are you? A machine for turning out opinions, like a pasta machine?*

Seriously, can I tell you what I think about your opinions? I said. My candid thoughts? For what they are worth?

Yes, let me have your thoughts.

For instance, it may choose to discard the rule that a player shall make only one move at a time. How might this look in practice? Instead of striving as in the past to evolve a single strain capable of overwhelming the host body's resistances, the virus may succeed in evolving a whole class of dissimilar strains simultaneously, analogous to making a number of chess moves at once, all over the board.

We assume that, as long as it is applied with enough tenacity, human reason must triumph (is fated to triumph) over other forms of purposive activity because human reason is the only form of reason there is, the only key that can unlock the codes by which the universe works. Human reason, we say, is universal reason.

She laughed. You think I am like Imelda? she said. She threw open the shoe cupboard. It held forty pairs of shoes, at a guess.

She likes to present herself as a Filipina, a little Filipina guest-worker. In fact she has never lived in the Philippines. Her father was an Australian diplomat who married a woman he met at a cocktail party in Manila, the soon-to-be divorced wife of a property developer. Until her father decamped with his secretary and opened a restaurant in Cassis (big scandal), Anya went to international schools all over the place (Washington, Cairo, Grenoble).

OK. This may sound brutal, but it isn't meant that way. There is a tone – I don't know the best word to describe it – a tone that really turns people off. A know-it-all tone. Everything is cut and dried: *I am the one with all the answers, here is how it is, don't argue, it won't get you anywhere.* I know that isn't how you are in real life, but that is how you come across, and it is not what you want. I wish you would cut it out. If you positively have to write about the world and how you see it, I wish you could find a better way.

But what if there are equally powerful modes of "thinking," that is, equally effective biochemical processes for getting to where your drives or desires incline you? What if the contest to see on whose terms warm-blooded life will continue on this planet does not prove human reason to be the winner? The recent successes of human reason in its long contest with virus thinking should not delude us, for it has held the upper hand a mere instant in evolutionary time. What if the tide turns; and what if the lesson contained in that turn of the tide is that human reason has met its match?

What benefit she derived from that international schooling is not clear. She speaks French with an accent the French probably find charming but has not heard of Voltaire. She thinks Kyoto is a misspelling of Tokyo.

Is that all?
No, I have more to say, but on a different subject.
Then may I first say a word in my defence?
Go ahead.

16. On competition

In athletics, in foot-races, it used to be the case that, when the judge at the finishing line could not tell who had won, he would declare a dead heat. The judge here stood for the common man – the common man with the keenest eye. When, in an athletic contest, the keenest common eye can discern no difference, then, we used to say, there is indeed no difference.

Alan must make a lot of money, I said, to finance all these purchases of yours. She shrugged. He likes me to look good, she said. He likes to show me off. Doesn't he mind that you are working for me? I asked. It is not ordinary work, she replied.

These are dark times. You can't expect me to write about them in a light manner. Not when what I have to say is heartfelt.

Can't I? I don't see why the darkness of the times means you have to get on a soapbox and lecture. And why are the times so dark anyway? I don't think these are dark times. I think they are pretty good times. So let us just say we have different feelings on that point. Now can I say something about terrorism? When you write about the terrorists, I think – candidly – you are a bit up in the clouds. A bit idealistic. A bit unrealistic. My guess is you have never in your life come face to face with a real Muslim fundamentalist. Speak up, tell me if I am wrong. No? Well, I have, and I can tell you, they are not like you and me. Listen to what I am saying.

Similarly, in a game like cricket, the understanding used to be that when the umpire said that something had happened – the ball had touched the bat, for example – then for the purposes of the game it had indeed happened. Such understandings were in accord with the somewhat fictive character accorded to sporting contests: sport is not life; what "really" happens in sport does not really matter; what matters instead is what we agree has happened.

Today, however, the outcomes of contests are decided by devices keener than the keenest human eye: electronic cameras divide each second into a hundred instants and save each instant in its frozen image.

The handover of the power of decision to machines shows how far the nature of athletic contests, whose model used to be children's play – the contestants *played* at being foes – and whose modus

---

If it was ordinary work he would say it was a waste of resources. But typing for a celebrity writer, that is different. Ostentatiously she wiped her brow. It's hot, she said. I am going to change.

I have an uncle, my mother's brother, who owns a timber mill on Mindanao. The Islamists on Mindanao campaigned against the mill, they said they wanted it closed down, it was stealing their resources, the island's resources. My uncle refused. He wasn't stealing anything, he said, he had legal title. So one night the Islamists arrived in force. They shot the mill manager in front of his wife and children, they set fire to the processing plant and watched while it burned down. In the name of Allah. In the name of the Prophet. That is Mindanao. It is the same in Bali, the same in Malaysia, the same everywhere where the fundamentalists get a toehold. You saw for yourself what they did in Bali.

74

operandi used to be consensus, has been reconceived. What used to be play has now become work, and decisions about who wins and who loses have become potentially too important – that is to say, too costly – to be left to the fallible human eye.

The lead in this anti-social, anti-human turn was taken by horseracing, which despite being known as the sport of kings always had a questionable standing in the gallery of sports, both because the contestants were not human beings and because races were so nakedly a vehicle for betting. Simply put, deciding the result of a horserace was left to the camera because so much money rode on the result.

The abandonment of the old, "natural" ways of adjudicating in sport in favour of new, mechanical ways paralleled a larger-scale historical development: from sporting competition as a recreation

---

Excuse me. And she shooed me out of the dressing room but then left the door open so that if I had turned around (but I did not) I could have watched her slipping out of her jeans and into the same tomato-red house-smock in which she had first appeared to me.

You are wasting your pity on the fundamentalists, Mister C. They despise your pity. They aren't like you. They don't believe in talking, in reasoning. They don't want to be clever. They despise being clever. They prefer to be stupid, deliberately stupid. You can argue with them all you like, it has no effect. They have made up their minds. They know what they know, they don't need to know anything more. And they are not afraid. They don't mind dying if it helps to bring the day of reckoning nearer.

The day of reckoning?

The day of the battle to end all battles, when the infidels are defeated and Islam takes over the world.

for healthy young males (and to a lesser extent females), which members of the public with time to spare could, if they felt so inclined, watch for free, to sport as an entertainment staged for masses of paying spectators by businessmen employing professional contestants. Here professional boxing provided the model, and long before boxing gladiatorial contests.

To the generation brought up under the new dispensation, laments over what has been lost are as uninteresting as laments for the demise of the wood-frame tennis racquet. Should the Jeremiahs therefore shut up? The obvious answer is Yes. Is there any sense in which the answer might be No?

In sport, even modern sport, we look forward to equal contests. A contest whose outcome is a foregone conclusion does not engage us, save perhaps when the weaker contestant performs bravely

---

This flat gets so hot in summer, she said, when she rejoined me. It's because of the height. You don't want to exchange flats, just for the summer? I bet it's cooler lower down.

I think you are confusing Muslims with Christians. It is the Christian fundamentalists who look forward to the battle to end all battles. They call it Armageddon. They look forward to Armageddon and the inauguration of the universal reign of the Christian God. That is why they are so reckless about going to war. That is why they are so indifferent to the future of the planet. This isn't our home, they say to themselves: Heaven is our home.

Well, there you go, giving everything a political twist again. I try to tell you what real-life fundamentalists are like, and you turn it into a boxing match, your opinion versus my opinion, Muslims versus Christians. As I told you, it soon gets boring. But you probably like boxing – you and the terrorists. I don't. Boxing leaves me cold.

enough to win our sympathetic admiration. For to face up bravely to a stronger rival is of course one of the lessons that sport, as a cultural institution, was invented to teach.

The confrontation between a nostalgic, backward-looking view of sport and the view that predominates today may have an analogous cultural value. That is to say, the argument that the past was better than the present cannot be won, but at least it can be bravely put.

*

Two.

Given that food is abundant in Australia and the climate congenial, why do Australians need to be urged – by a government that has just passed new laws to make it easier for employers to fire employees –

She says silly things like that (of course she is not really proposing an exchange of units) without the slightest embarrassment. I will show you my photo album, she offered the other day.

Then let us change the subject. If boxing leaves you cold, and politics leaves you even colder, what makes you hot?

Aha, I thought to myself, *that is what you are interested in, is it – what makes me hot!* I enjoy a good story, I said coolly. I told you. A story with human interest, that I can relate to. There is nothing wrong with that.

*

Alan and I talked about him again last night. He told me one of his dreams, I said to Alan. It was really sad, about dying and his ghost lingering behind, not wanting to leave. I told him he should write it down before he forgets, and work it into his book.

to work harder and for longer hours? The answer we are given is that in the new, globalized economy we will all have to work harder to *stay ahead*, or indeed even to *keep pace*. The Chinese work longer hours for less pay than Australians, we are told, and live meaner and more cramped lives. Thus China is able to manufacture goods more cheaply than Australia. Unless Australians work harder, they will *fall behind* and become *losers* in the great global race.

Behind this rebuke to the otiose life (*otium*: leisure time which may or may not be used for self-improvement) and justification of unceasing business lie assumptions that no longer need to be articulated, so self-evidently true do they seem: that each person on earth must belong to one nation or another and operate within one or other national economy; that these national economies are in competition with one another.

I did not take her up on it. I have no wish to see the adored, spoiled, and probably vain girl-child she must have been.
This year, the year when her comet-path crosses mine, marks her apogee. Another decade and her body will begin to thicken,

---

No, he said, he couldn't do that: it had to be an opinion to belong in his book, and a dream isn't an opinion. Then you should find someplace where it will fit, I told him (I told Alan). It's a good dream, a high-quality dream with a beginning and a middle and an end. My own dreams never make sense. And by the way (I asked Alan), who is Eurydice? She was in the dream.

Orpheus and Eurydice, said Alan, famous lovers. Orpheus was the man, Eurydice was the woman who got turned into a pillar of salt.

I am beginning to feel sorry for him, I said. He's got no one. Sits in his flat all day, or in the park talking to the birds.

Well, said Alan, there is always the bottle to fall back on when he gets too lonely.

What do you mean, there is always the bottle?

The figure of economic activity as a race or contest is somewhat vague in its particulars, but it would appear that, as a race, it has no finishing line and therefore no natural end. The runner's sole goal is to get to the front and stay there. The question of why life must be likened to a race, or of why the national economies must race against one another rather than going for a comradely jog together, for the sake of the health, is not raised. A race, a contest: that is the way things are. By nature we belong to separate nations; by nature nations are in competition with other nations. We are as nature made us. The world is a jungle (the metaphors proliferate), and in the jungle all species are in competition with all other species for space and sustenance.

---

her features to coarsen; she will become just another idle, overdressed woman needing to come to terms with the fact that men no longer spare her a glance in the street.

Didn't you tell me he is a secret drinker? Anyway, don't feel too sorry for him. Not everyone can manage to make a living turning their idle opinions into cash. It is ingenious, when you come to think of it, as a way of operating in both dimensions at the same time.

The two dimensions, the individual dimension and the economic dimension – that is how Alan sees the world, the individual dimension being nobody's business but your own and the economic dimension being the big picture. I probably agree, it makes a lot of sense, but I argue about it anyway, about whether that is all there is, and Alan argues back, so he can see for himself that the woman he dumped his wife for is not a dummy who happens to have a nice body, but someone with a mind of her own, someone with spunk, as he puts it (but not as much spunk as my lord and master, I usually reply).

The truth about jungles is that among the nations (the species) of the typical jungle there are no longer winners or losers: the losers became extinct ages ago. A jungle is an ecosystem where the surviving species have attained symbiosis with each other. This achieved state of dynamic stability is what it means to be an ecosystem.

But even aside from the dud analogy with the jungle, the claim that the world has to be divided into competing economies because that is the nature of the world is strained. If we have competing economies, we have them because we have decided that that is how we want our world to be. Competition is a sublimation of warfare.

Alan and I have been together for three years, she said. Before Alan I was with someone else, a Frenchman. He and I were engaged. His name was Luc. Lucky Luc. From Lyon. He was out here working in the wine trade. He told his mother of our marriage plans, sent her a picture of the two of us together,

---

So I say, But is Señor C really such a fraud? Don't we all have opinions that we try to extend into the real world? For example, I have opinions about colour and style, about what goes with what. So when I go to the shoe shop, I buy shoes that in my opinion match the dress I bought yesterday. As a result of that opinion the shoe shop makes money, the factory that made the shoes makes money, the importer that imported them, and so forth. How is that different from Señor C? Señor C has a dream about dying and wakes up in a state, wondering if there isn't something wrong with him. So he goes to his GP for a checkup. His GP makes money, his GP's receptionist, the laboratory that does the blood tests, etcetera, and all as the result of a dream. So what is the economic dimension, in the end, but the sum total of extensions from our individual dimensions, our dreams and opinions and so forth?

There is nothing ineluctable about war. If we want war we can choose war, if we want peace we can equally well choose peace. If we want competition we can choose competition; alternatively we can take the path of comradely collaboration.

What those people who trot out the jungle analogy really mean, but don't say because it sounds too pessimistic, too predestinarian, is: *homo homini lupus*. We cannot collaborate because human nature – leave aside the nature of the world – is fallen, vicious, predatory. (The poor, maligned beasts! The wolf is not predatory upon other wolves: *lupus lupo lupus* would be a slander.)

Luc and Anya. She threw a fit. She said she wasn't going to have two Cambodges in the family. Luc's older brother was already married to a girl from Cambodia, an air hostess. I said to Luc, Tell your mother I am not a Cambodge and while you are about it tell her to go to hell. And you can go to hell too. And that was that. End of Luc.

Good question, replies Alan. Except you forget one thing: that dreams about shoes can't extend into the economic dimension if you can't afford to buy shoes. Ditto anxiety dreams: anxiety can't enter the economic dimension if you can't do anything about your anxiety because you haven't got the money. But there is a more general point that you miss. (Alan loves it when he can say, *You miss the point* or *What you fail to see is*, and it gives me a kick too, sometimes, to see his excitement.) The datum has to start its life in the individual dimension, agreed, before it can migrate to the economic. But then something happens. Once a critical mass of data is reached, quantity becomes quality. So the economic not only sums up the individual, it also transcends it.

17. On intelligent design

A US court recently ruled that public schools in some town or other in Pennsylvania may not use science classes to teach the account of the universe known as Intelligent Design, and in specific may not teach Intelligent Design as an alternative to Darwinism.

I have no desire to associate myself with the people behind the Intelligent Design movement. Nevertheless, I continue to find evolution by random mutation and natural selection not just unconvincing but preposterous as an account of how complex organisms come into being. As long as there is not one of us who has the faintest idea of how to go about constructing a housefly from scratch, how can we disparage as intellectually naïve the conclusion that the housefly must have been put together by an intelligence of a higher order than our own? If anyone in the picture is naïve, it is the person who elevates the operating rules of Western science into epistemological axioms, arguing that what cannot be demonstrated scientifically to be true (or, to use the more timid word preferred by science, *valid*) cannot be true (valid), not just by the standard of truth (validity) used by practitioners of science but by any standard that counts.

You have quite a temper, I said. She took it as a compliment.

Why does she keep reminding me she is not married? I could offer her my hand, my hand and my fortune: *Dump Alan, be mine!* Would I be mad enough to take that plunge?

Still, I say, putting on my crestfallen look, backtracking, preparing to accept defeat (I learned long ago it is not worth the candle to get into an argument with Alan and win), I feel sorry for the old man (by which Alan understands me to mean, *As a woman I claim my natural right to be soft-hearted*). That is OK, says Alan, as long as you don't let your feelings run away with you. *That is OK,* meaning, *I understand, I know you can't help it, I wouldn't want you to be otherwise, it is part of your feminine charm.*

It does not seem to me philosophically retrograde to attribute intelligence to the universe as a whole, rather than just to a subset of mammals on planet Earth. An intelligent universe evolves purposively over time, even if the purpose in question may for ever be beyond the grasp of the human intellect and indeed beyond the range of our idea of what might constitute purpose.

Insofar as one might want to go further and distinguish a universal intelligence from the universe as a whole – a step I see no reason to take – one might want to give that intelligence the handy monosyllabic name *God.* But even if one were to take that step, one would still be very far from positing – and embracing – a God who demanded to be believed in, a God who had any interest in our thoughts about it ("him"), or a God who rewarded good deeds and punished evildoers.

I went off the rails once, she said. Temporarily. Alan rescued me. That is how I got to know him.

I recollected myself and waited to hear how she had gone off the rails.

Alan is very good that way, she said. Very stable. Very fatherly. Perhaps because he didn't have a father himself. Did you know that?

We argue a lot, Alan and I, yet in bed we get on like a house on fire. We could become famous lovers one day. A good argument keeps the mind sharp, says Alan. I learn a lot from him too. He is always reading, always going to seminars and presentations on the latest thinking. He reads the *Wall Street Journal* and *The Economist* online, he has subscriptions to *The National Interest* and *Quadrant.* The partners kid him for being too much of an intellectual. But it is all good-humoured, he is always ahead of the market, they respect him for that.

When we first got together he didn't know much about sex, about what a woman wants, which was funny, considering he was a married man. But I coaxed him along, coached him along, and now he is up with the best. There is a fire in him that is always burning for me, and a woman can excuse a lot in return for that.

People who claim that behind every feature of every organism lies a history of selection from random mutation should try to answer the following question: Why is it that the intellectual apparatus that has evolved for human beings seems to be incapable of comprehending *in any degree of detail* its own complexity? Why do we human beings typically experience awe – a recoil of the mind, as if before an abyss – when we try to comprehend, *grasp*, certain things, such as the origin of space and time, the being of nothingness, the nature of understanding itself? I cannot see what evolutionary advantage this combination gives us – the combination of insufficiency of intellectual grasp together with consciousness that the grasp is insufficient.

I know nothing about Alan, I said.

He was an orphan. He was brought up in an orphanage. He had to make his own way. He is an interesting man. You should get to know him.

Rule Two: Never have anything to do with the husband. You went off the rails, I said.

Mister Rabbit, I call him sometimes, Mister Jackrabbit. Once we did it four times in a single afternoon. Is that a record or is that a record, he said after the fourth time. It is a record, I said. Mister Rabbit. Mister Carrot Top. Mister Big.

By the way, I say, Señor C has been inquiring about financial planning. Sure, says Alan, I will take care of him. What kind of care will you take? I ask. Good care, he says. What kind of care is good care? I ask. Ask no questions and you will be told no lies, he replies. I don't want you to make a fool of him, I say. I won't make a fool of him, he says, *au contraire* I will be his guardian angel. He is old and sad, I say, he can't help what he feels for me, just as you can't help what you feel for me. You don't have to tell me, he says. My Princess of Pussy. My Queen of Cunt. Don't hurt him, I say. Promise. Promise, he says.

Eugène Marais, who belonged to the first generation to thoroughly absorb Darwinian doctrine, wondered in what evolutionary direction he himself might be pointing, whether he might not be an instance of a mutation that was not going to prosper, and might therefore in that sense be doomed to extinction. In fact people like Marais wondered whether the whole strain within mankind that they represented, characterized by hyper-development of the intellect, was not a doomed evolutionary experiment, marking a route that mankind as a whole could not and would not follow. Thus their answer to the question above was: An intellectual apparatus marked by a conscious knowledge of its insufficiency is an evolutionary aberration.

Yes. But I have been leading a quiet life since then. How about you? Have you ever been off the rails?

No, I said, I don't believe I have. And it is too late now. If I went off the rails at my age I wouldn't have time to get back on.

Do I believe Alan? Of course I don't believe him, and he doesn't for a moment think I believe him. There is the individual dimension, and then there is the bigger picture. A lie in the individual dimension does not necessarily count as a lie in the bigger picture. It can transcend its origins. I don't need Alan to teach me that. It's like makeup. Makeup may be a lie, but not if everyone wears it. If everyone wears makeup, makeup becomes the way things are, and what is the truth but the way things are?

18. On Zeno

How do we count? How do we learn to count? Is what we do when we count the same as what we do when we learn to count?

There are two methods of teaching a child to count. One is to lay down a row of buttons (How long a row? – That remains to be settled) and ask the child to move from left to right, first putting the forefinger of one hand (one hand only) on the leftmost button and at the same time uttering a word (*nomen,* name) – in English *one* – from a given list, then putting the finger on the next button and uttering the next name from the list, *two,* and so on *until the child gets the idea* (what the idea is will be taken up later), at which point the child can be said to have learned to count. The list of names referred to varies from language to language, but in all cases is understood to be unendingly long.

That's lucky, she said. A pause. You have no idea what kind of person I am, do you? she said.

Alan believes that because Señor C has wicked thoughts about me he qualifies for correction, six of the best with a cane across his scrawny buttocks (Alan hasn't actually put it in words, but I know I am right). But are wicked thoughts really so wicked, I ask myself, when you are too old to put them into practice and keep them locked up in their own dimension anyway? For an old man, after all, what is there left in the world but wicked thoughts? Señor C can't help it if he desires me, just as I can't help it if I am desired. Besides, Alan likes other men to look at me. He won't admit it, but I know it is true. You are mine, aren't you, he says when he has me in his arms. Aren't you? Aren't you? And he presses my wrists so hard that it hurts. Yours, always yours, I gasp, and he comes, and then I come. That is the way things are between us. Hot as fire.

*

The second method is to put one button down before the child and ask her to utter the first name (*one*) from the list, then to put another button down and ask her to utter the next name (*two*), then to put another button down, and so forth, until the child *gets the idea*.

The child gets the idea by induction, but what is the idea? The idea is that, although the list is unending (and therefore unmemorizable, unlearnable), individual new names in it are quite few in number; furthermore that the list is ordered and has a system, with individual names being combined and recombined according to a rule, a rule that will tell you how, given the name of the number of the button on which you now have your finger, you can predict the name of the next button (teaching method one); or that will tell you how, given the last name you have uttered, to predict what name you should utter when the next button falls (teaching method two).

No, I don't, I said. She was right. The very same thought had in fact just crossed my mind: that while I had a very clear sense of her physical being, both as it was now and as it would be in the future, as one might have the clearest sense of a flower – its radiance, its brave upthrust, its weight in the world – I had no real grasp of what went on in the mind of this woman with whom

---

Among Señor C's latest set of opinions there is one that disturbs me, makes me wonder if I have misjudged him all along. It is about sex with children. He doesn't exactly come out in favour of it, but he doesn't come out against it either. I ask myself, Is this his way of saying his appetites run in that direction? Because why would he write about it otherwise?

I can understand that he should have the hots for a petite number like me. Lots of men are like that. I would be the same if I was a man. But little girls are a different story. I saw enough of old men and little girls in Viet Nam, more than enough.

In English-language societies, which use the near-universal decimal system of counting, the rule tells you that you need memorize only twelve names (*one, two, . . . eleven, twelve*), in sequence, after which you can *work out* (to be glossed either as *construct* or else as *predict*) how the list of names goes on. But even this is an extravagant requirement. In theory you can manage with only two names, *one* and *two*, or with a single name, *one*, plus a concept, adding (adding one to something).

There is another, more concise, language-independent way of telling the same story using not the names of numbers but the abstract symbols (abstract in the sense of being tied to no phonic token) *1, 2, 3* . . . But the price of that concision is losing contact with the voice of the learner reciting in order from the list as she touches the buttons.

– out of my own boredom, no doubt, my own idleness, my own empty-headedness – I seem to have grown obsessed, to the extent that a man can be called obsessed when the sexual urge has dwindled and there is only a hovering uncertainty about what he is actually after, what he actually expects the object of his infatuation to supply.

His argument – which seems to be about pornography but behind that is about sex – goes as follows. Filming a man having sex with a twelve-year-old, an actual twelve-year-old, should be prohibited, he has no quarrel with that, since sex with a child, whether in front of a camera or not, is a criminal act. But a seventeen-year-old pretending to be a twelve-year-old is completely different. When a sex scene is done with actors who are legally of consenting age it suddenly becomes art, and art is OK.

My first reaction is to go back to him and say, How do you know an actor who looks like a child and acts the part of a child isn't in fact a child? Since when have movie credits come with everyone's ages in brackets behind their names, and notarized copies of their birth certificates? Get real!

From the moment when the learner *gets it*, namely gets the rule for naming the next number, the whole of mathematics takes off. The whole of mathematics rests on my ability to *count* – my ability, given the name of N, to name N+1 without knowing its name beforehand, without memorizing an infinite list. Much of mathematics consists of clever stratagems for recasting situations where I can't count (can't work out the name of the next element of the series – the name of the next irrational number, for instance) in terms of situations where I can count.

Most practising mathematicians practise mathematics on the understanding that we construct the numbers as we go: given *one* we construct *two* by applying the rule *add one to the given number*,

---

That is the advantage of being a humble typist. And then, as if reading my mind, she said: While she gets to study her Señor into his inmost depths, her Señor knows nothing of what is going on in her.

I made Alan listen to the tape, and Alan at once put his finger on the weak link. Alan is very quick, he cuts through the crap in no time. He is trying to draw a line between realities and perceptions, said Alan. But everything is a perception. That is what Kant proved. That was the Kantian revolution. We simply don't have access to the noumenal. So the whole of life is a set of perceptions, finally. And movies are the same, only in spades – twenty-four perceptions per second, through a mechanical eye. If the audience in a theatre perceives a child being raped, then it is a child being raped, period, social consensus, end of story. And if it is a child being raped, then boom!, you go to the slammer, you and your financial backers and your director and your whole crew, all the participants in the crime – that is the law, in black and white. Whereas if the audience isn't taken in, if the actress has big tits and is clearly a grown-up faking it, then it is a different story, then it is just a failed movie.

one; then we construct *three* by applying the rule to two; and so on indefinitely. The numbers are not there waiting to be found (waiting to be reached as the counting process proceeds): by following the rule we effectively construct them out of thin air, one after another, without end.

The names of the numbers are thus not quite like words in a language, even though they seem to belong to the language. The dictionary of the language already hints that the names of numbers are not proper words by listing only a handful of them. In no English-language dictionary, for example, will we find an entry for the word *twenty-three*. Normal words, unlike the names of numbers, are put together out of sounds more or less arbitrarily chosen.

Tread carefully, I said. You may be seeing less of my inmost depths than you believe. The opinions you happen to be typing do not necessarily come from my inmost depths.

So if you make good child pornography – I mean convincing pornography – you go to jail, and if you make bad child pornography you don't – is that it? I said.

That is about the sum of it, says Alan, that is the risk you take. You make a failed movie and you make no money but you don't go to jail. You make a good movie and potentially you make lots of money, only you go to jail. You balance the pluses against the minuses and decide. That is how everything works, pluses and minuses. Natural justice.

I would like to bring Alan and Señor C together to debate the paedophilia business. Alan would wipe the floor with him. Even I could wipe the floor with him if I wanted to. I would wipe the floor with him and then march out. *Do you think I am a dummy?* I would say. *Do you think I can't read between the lines? Keep your money, I don't need it, do your own typing.* Grand exit. Curtain.

Thus it would make little difference to the English language if the word *krap* were to replace the work *park* wherever *park* occurred. Mathematics, on the other hand, would be thrown into confusion if *3618* were to replace *8163* wherever *8163* occurred (e.g. 8162 + 1 = 3618; 907 x 9 = 3618). There are, it must be conceded, some rudimentary rules of word-formation in language itself – rules with hosts of exceptions – that enable us to foretell from a verb, for example, what the related noun, adjective, and adverb will be (*act – action – active – actively*); but there is nothing as extensive as the counting rule, the rule that enables us to foretell (or construct or discover) new words (new names of numbers) indefinitely.

The thesis that the numbers are constructed by us as we count faces certain obstacles. For instance, we can show that there are indefinitely many prime numbers. However, given the Nth prime,

---

"Dishonour descends upon one's shoulders," she repeated softly. That sounds like the inmost depths to me.

I sat shaken, speechless.

So what is going to save you from dishonour, Señor C? she said. And when I did not respond: Who are you expecting to rescue you?

I don't know, I said. If I knew I wouldn't be so lost.

I am willing to bet Señor C has a stash of pornography somewhere in the flat. I should check the bookshelves, see whether maybe there aren't one or two *verboten* videotapes hidden behind the books. *Emmanuelle Four!* I would say – *I wonder what that is about. And Russian Dolls XXX! I used to have Russian dolls when I was a little girl in pigtails. Can I borrow them? I'll bring them back in a day or two.* What would he say to that? He would squirm. *Those tapes are research material,* he would lie, *for a book I am writing. Research?* I would say. *You mean scientific research? I didn't know you were a sexologist, Señor C.*

He is a leftover from the Sixties, that is all he is, says Alan. An old-fashioned free-love, free-speech sentimental hippie socialist,

we have no rule for constructing the $(N+1)^{th}$ prime; nor do we know how long we would have to go on testing numbers for primeness before we can be sure we will have reached it. In other words, the $(N+1)^{th}$ prime exists, therefore it must be constructible, but we do not know for sure how to say what its name will be within the lifetime of the universe.

But to take the alternative route, to say that the numbers are not constructed by us but are already there, waiting for us to find our way to them and plant markers (names) on them, raises even more daunting problems. My counting rule may enable me to plod successfully from 1 to N, naming (counting off) each number as I reach it, but who is to say that the button waiting for me to the immediate right of the button named N is indeed the button named N+1?

Well, your little Filipina typist can't do it for you. Your little Filipina typist with her shopping bags and her empty head.

I never said you had an empty head.

No, that's true, you never said so, you were too polite for that; but you thought so. You thought so from the first minute. *What a pretty ass,* you thought, *one of the prettiest asses I have ever seen. But nothing upstairs. If only I was younger,* you thought, *how I would love to bang her.* Confess. That was what you thought.

---

sentimental because there was nothing left of socialism except the flavour after the Berlin Wall came down and we got to see that the Soviet Union wasn't a world-historical empire, just a huge toxic dump with dinosaur factories grinding out shoddy goods no one wanted. But Mr C and his comrades from the Sixties refuse to open their eyes. They can't afford to, it would destroy their last illusions. They prefer to get together and drink pilsener and wave the red flag and sing the Internationale and reminisce about the good old days when they manned the barricades. Wake up! – you should tell him that. The world moves on. A new century. No more cruel bosses and starving workers. No more artificial divisions. We are all in this together.

This is the dark possibility at the heart of the paradoxes of Zeno. Before the arrow can reach its target, says Zeno, it must get half-way there; before it can get half-way it must get a quarter of the way; and so forth: $1, \frac{1}{2}, \frac{1}{4}, \ldots \frac{1}{2}^N, \frac{1}{2}^{(N+1)}, \ldots$ If we grant that the series of markers it needs to pass on its way to the target is infinitely long, then how can the arrow ever get there?

By inventing a way of summing the infinite number of infinitesimal steps on the way to the target and reaching a finite total, Isaac Newton believed he had overcome Zeno's paradox. But there are depths to the paradox that go beyond Newton. What if, in the interval between the newly attained N^{th} step and the never yet attained – never attained in the history of the universe – $(N+1)^{th}$, the arrow were to lose its way, fall into a hole, vanish?

Jorge Luis Borges wrote a poker-faced philosophical fable, "Funes the Memorious," about a man to whom the counting rule, and indeed the even more fundamental rules that allow us to encompass the world in language, are simply alien. Through an immense,

---

Approximately. That was approximately what I thought, though not in those terms.

That's okay, she said, I am used to it. It is not as if you tried to rape me. It is not as if you whispered lewd words in my ear. You are too polite for that. That would count as going off the rails, to you. And now dishonour descends on your shoulders, and you don't know how to get rid of it.

Without wishing to split hairs, I say, isn't he more of an anarchist than a socialist? Socialists want the state to run everything, don't they? Whereas he keeps saying the state is a gang of bandits.

Which is true, says Alan. I don't disagree with that aspect of his analysis. And the more state intervention you have, the more banditry. Look at Africa. Africa will never get going economically because all you have there are bandit state apparatuses backed by bandit armies, collecting tribute from business and from the population. That is the root of your guy's problem: Africa.

solitary intellectual effort, Funes constructs a counting that is not a system of counting, a counting that makes no assumptions about what comes next after N. By the time Borges' narrator meets him, Funes has advanced as far as what ordinary people would call the number twenty-four thousand.

> In place of seven thousand [and] thirteen, he would say (for example) *Máximo Pérez*; in place of seven thousand [and] fourteen, *The Railroad*; other numbers were *Luis Melián Lafinur, Olimar, sulphur, the reins, the whale, gas, the cauldron, Napoleon, Agustín de Vedia.* In place of five hundred, he would say *nine* . . . I tried to explain to him that this rhapsody of incoherent terms was precisely the opposite of a system of numbers. I told him that saying 365 meant saying three hundreds, six tens, five units, an analysis which is not to be found in the "numbers" *The Negro Timoteo* or *meat blanket.* Funes did not understand me or refused to understand me.[6]

You are mixing up two things, I said. Two different sources of shame, of two different grades.

Maybe I do, maybe I mix up different sources. Are there really different kinds of shame, though? I thought it was all the same, once it settled in. But I defer to you, you are the expert, you are the one who knows. What are you going to do about your kind of shame?

That is where he came from, that is where he is stuck, mentally. In his mind he can't get away from Africa.

He is not my guy, I say.

Everywhere he looks he sees Africa, he sees banditry, says Alan, who is not listening to me. He doesn't understand modernity. He doesn't understand the managerial state.

Which is not a bandit state, I say.

Alan gives me a funny look. Are you falling under his influence? he says. Whose side are you on?

Borges' kabbalistic, Kantian fable brings it home to us that the order we see in the universe may not reside in the universe at all, but in the paradigms of thought we bring to it. The mathematics we have invented (in some accounts) or discovered (in others), which we believe or hope to be a key to the structure of the universe, may equally well be a private language – private to human beings with human brains – in which we doodle on the walls of our cave.

I don't know, I said. I have no idea. I was going to say (I said) that when you live in shameful times shame descends upon you, shame descends upon everyone, and you have simply to bear it, it is your lot and your punishment. Am I wrong? Enlighten me.

Let me tell you a story, she said. It may help, it may not. I was in Cancún a few years ago, on the Yucatan, travelling with a girl friend. We were sitting in a bar having a drink and we got into conversation with these American college boys, and they invited us to come and have a look at their boat. They seemed nice, so what the hell, we went with them. Then they said, How about we go for a sail?

I am not falling under his influence. I just want to hear a simple explanation for why the managerial state is not a bandit state.

OK, I will explain. The state is brought into being to protect its citizens. That is why it exists: to provide security while we get on with our life-activities, which taken all together and *aufgehoben* constitute the economy. The state wraps a shield around the economy. Also, for the time being, for lack of a better agency, it makes macro-economic decisions when they need to be made, and enforces them; but that is another story for another day.

19. On probability

Einstein famously said that God does not play with dice. He was expressing a belief (a faith? a hope?) that the laws governing the universe have a deterministic rather than a probabilistic character.

To most physicists today, Einstein's notion of what constitutes a physical law seems a little naïve. Nevertheless, Einstein is a formidable ally to call upon for those whose suspicions about probabilistic statements and their explanatory value will not go away.

Well, they took us for a sail, and I won't go into the details but there were three of them and two of us, and they must have decided we were just a couple of bimbos, a couple of *putas*, whereas they were sons of doctors and lawyers and what have you, they were taking us cruising on the Caribbean, so we owed them, so they could do what they liked with us. Three of them. Three strapping young males.

Shielding the economy is not banditry, Anya. It can degenerate into banditry, but structurally it is not banditry. Your Señor C's problem is that he can't think structurally. Everywhere he looks he wants to see personal motives at work. He wants to see cruelty. He wants to see greed and exploitation. It is all a morality play to him, good versus evil. What he fails to see or refuses to see is that individuals are players in a structure that transcends individual motives, transcends good and evil. Even the guys in Canberra and the state capitals, who may indeed be bandits at a personal level – I am ready to concede the point there – who may be peddling influence and stealing nuts on the side and storing them up for their personal future, even those guys work within the system, whether they are aware of it or not.

For instance, here is a proposition of a loose kind such as we encounter every day: that overweight men are at increased risk of heart attack. What does this proposition mean, strictly speaking? It means that if you weigh hundreds or thousands of men of the same age and divide them into two classes, overweight and not over-weight ("normal"), using some or other agreed-upon criterion for what constitutes overweight, and follow their case histories over time, you will find that the number of overweight men who have suffered heart attacks by a certain age is proportionately higher than the number of "normal" men who have suffered heart attacks; and even if the number for the particular group of men you are studying does *not* in fact turn out to be greater, if you repeat the investigation many times in different places with different men over different time periods, the number *will* turn out to be greater; and

---

We didn't return to port at all that day. The second day out at sea my girl friend broke down and tried to jump overboard, and that gave them a fright, so they put in at some little fishing village down the coast and dumped us there. The end of one little adventure, they thought, now let's go look for another one.

Within the market, I say.

Within the market, if you like. Which is beyond good and evil, like Nietzsche said. Good motives or evil motives, they are just motives in the end, vectors of the matrix, that get evened out in the long run. But your guy doesn't see that. He comes from another world, another era. The modern world is beyond him. The phenom-enon of the modern United States is wholly beyond him. He looks at the US and all he sees is a battle between good and evil, the evil Bush–Cheney–Rumsfeld axis on the one hand and the good terrorists on the other along with their friends the cultural relativists.

And Australia? I said. What is there about Australia that is beyond him?

even if the number is *not yet* greater, if you doggedly go on repeating the investigation often enough it *will* eventually become greater.

If you ask the investigator how he or she can be sure that the numbers will eventually come right and thus that the claimed cause-and-effect relation between overweight and heart attack will be proven, your question will be rephrased and answered in the following terms: "I am ninety-five per cent sure," or "I am ninety-eight per cent sure." What does it mean to be ninety-five per cent sure? you may ask. "It means I will be right in at least nineteen cases out of twenty; or, if not in nineteen out of twenty, then in nineteen thousand out of twenty thousand," the investigator will reply. And which case is the present one, you ask: the nineteenth or the twentieth, the nineteen-thousandth or the twenty-thousandth?

But they were wrong. It wasn't the end. We got back to Cancún and we laid charges with the police, we had all the names, all the particulars, and they issued a warrant and those boys were arrested at the next port where they stopped and their yacht was impounded and the story hit the papers back in Connecticut or wherever and they were in deep shit.

He doesn't understand Australian politics. He looks around for big issues and when he doesn't see any he pronounces judgment on us: Australians are narrow-minded, insular, callous (for proof, look at the case of poor David Hicks), and as for our politics, it is without content, just personality contests and slanging-matches. Well, of course there are no big issues in Australia. There are no big issues in any modern state, not any more. That is what defines modernity. The big issues, the issues that count, have been settled. Even the politicians know that in their hearts. Politics is no longer where the action is. Politics is a sideshow. And your man ought to be grateful for that, not dour and disapproving like he is. If he wants old-fashioned politics, where people stage coups and murder each other and there is no security and everyone keeps their money under their pillow, he should go back to Africa. He will be completely at home there.

Which case is the present one? Which case am *I*? What does your claim about eating too much and the consequences of eating too much mean for *me*? *If* I want to avoid a heart attack *then* I should eat moderately – that is the lesson I am supposed to draw. But am I being assured that *if* I eat moderately *then* I will not have a heart attack? No. God plays dice. It is not in the nature of probabilistic claims that they can be disconfirmed by example. They can be confirmed or disconfirmed only probabilistically, by other statistical investigations conducted on other masses of subjects; and disconfirmation can occur only in the form, "The claim that overweight men are at increased risk of heart attack cannot be sustained on probabilities and is therefore in that sense probably not valid."

How do people respond in real life to being told that if they eat too much they will "be at increased risk" of heart attack? One response is: "What is the point of living if I cannot enjoy my food?"

So why am I telling you this story? Because when we went to the police, the *jefe*, the police captain, a very nice man, very sympathetic, said to us, You are sure you want to do this (meaning, are you sure you want this story to get out), because, you know, dishonour, *infamia*, is like bubble gum, wherever it touches it sticks.

Alan is forty-two. I am twenty-nine. It is Friday evening. We could be out having a good time. Instead, what are we doing? We are sitting alone, drinking beer, watching the traffic on the sliver of Darling Harbour that is all we can see between the high-rises, discussing the old man on the ground floor, whether he is a socialist or an anarchist. Or rather, we are sitting alone and Alan is telling me what's what about the old man on the ground floor. I am not criticizing Alan, but we have no social life. Alan doesn't like my friends from before I met him, and he has no friends of his own except business colleagues, whom he says he sees enough of during the week. So here we are like a pair of lonely old crows on a branch.

Don't you think we are spending too much time on Señor C? I say.

I couldn't agree more, says Alan. What do you want to talk about instead?

meaning that in a calculus of advantage and disadvantage, a short, fat life is preferable to a long, thin life. Another is, "My grandfather was fat and he lived to be ninety," meaning, "You propose this as a law that holds for all men, yet I have already disconfirmed it by example." My own response is: "I don't understand the phrase *at increased risk*. Please paraphrase it in simpler language, language that does not include such abstract terms as *chance, probability*." (Can't be done.)

Probabilistic propositions constitute a little world unto themselves. What is stated in probabilistic terms can be interpreted only in probabilistic terms. If you do not already think in probabilistic terms, predictions emerging out of the probabilistic world seem vacuous. Can one imagine the Sphinx foretelling that Oedipus will probably kill his father and marry his mother? Can one imagine Jesus saying that he will probably come again?

You know what I said? I said, This is the twentieth century, *capitano* (it was still the twentieth century then). In the twentieth century, when a man rapes a woman it is the man's dishonour.

I don't want to talk, I say. I want to do something.

We could go to a movie, says Alan. If there is anything worth seeing. Do you want to do that?

If you like, I say. What I don't say is: Can't we do something new for a change?

Señor C has opinions about God and the universe and everything else. He records his opinions (drone drone) which I dutifully type out (clickety clack) and somewhere down the line the Germans buy his book and pore over it (*ja ja*). As for Alan, Alan sits all day hunched over his computer and then comes home and tells me his opinions about interest rates and Macquarie Bank's latest moves, to which I dutifully listen. But what about me? Who listens to my opinions?

What am I failing to take into account when I talk like this? That the probabilistic laws of quantum physics give us a better way of understanding the universe than the old deterministic ones, better because the substance of the universe is in some sense indeterminate and the laws are therefore by their nature in better accord with reality? That the mode of thinking about the relation between present and future typified by foretelling depends on an archaic time sense?

What would life be like if one were to strike out *every* rule that can be stated only in probabilistic terms? "If you bet on such-and-such a horse you will probably lose your money." "If you drive above the speed limit you will probably be arrested." "If you make a play for her you will probably be turned down." The colloquial term for discounting probabilities is *taking risks*. Who is to say that a life of risk-taking isn't (probably?) better than a life lived by the rules?

The dishonour sticks to the man, not to the woman. At least that is how it is where I come from. And we signed the papers, my friend and me, and we walked out.

And? I said.

There is something else nagging at me. Alan says Señor C says Australians have grown callous, as proved by their indifference to the plight of David Hicks. Well, Señor C never mentions David Hicks until the instalment I typed yesterday, an instalment I have never discussed with Alan (haven't had a chance). So how come Alan knows about David Hicks? Is he going through my files behind my back? And why would he be doing that?

20. On raiding

The generation of white South Africans before my own, the generation of my parents, was witness to a significant moment in history, when people from the old, tribal Africa began to migrate en masse to cities and towns in search of work, settling there and having children there. That epochal moment my parents' generation misread in a calamitous way. Without reflecting, they assumed that African children born in the cities had somehow to carry the memory of that migration within themselves, to have an inward consciousness of themselves as a pivotal, transitional generation between an old and a new Africa, and to see their urban surroundings as fresh, unfamiliar, amazing – as Europe's great gift to Africa.

But life is not like that. The world into which we are born, each of us, is *our* world. Trains, cars, tall buildings (three generations back), mobile telephones, cheap clothing, fast food (present generation) – these constitute the world *as it is*, unquestioned, certainly not a gift from strangers, a gift to be marvelled at and felt thankful for.

And nothing. That's all. The rest doesn't concern you. When you tell me you walk around bent under your load of dishonour, I think of those girls from the old days who had the bad luck to get raped and then had to wear black for the rest of their lives – wear black and sit in a corner and never go to parties and never get married.

What do you think of what Señor C says about science, I ask Alan – about numbers and about Einstein and so forth?

Alan isn't a scientist, his degree is in business, but he has become a whiz at mathematical modelling, he has given seminars on it. He reads a lot, knows about lots of things.

The city-born child bears no mark of the bush. There is no "painful transition to modernity" to be undergone. The black children whom my parents patronized were more modern than they, who had themselves as young people migrated from farms and rural backwaters to the cities and still retained the manners of a country upbringing.

Nor was I immune from their error. During the years when Cape Town was my home, I thought of it as "my" city not just because I had been born there but above all because I knew the history of the place deeply enough to see its past in palimpsest beneath its present. But to the bands of young blacks who roam its streets today looking for action, it is "their" city and I am the outsider. History has no life unless you give it a home in your consciousness; it is a load no free person can be forced to take on.

People see what they call a crime wave sweeping the new South Africa, and shake their heads. What is the country coming to, they say. But the wave is anything but new. When they installed themselves on the land three centuries ago, settlers from north-western Europe opened themselves to the same practice of raiding (raiding of livestock, raiding of women) that marked relations between bands or tribes already resident there. Raiding, in southern Africa of early colonial times, had a peculiar conceptual status.

You have got it wrong, Mister C. Old thinking. Wrong analysis, as Alan would say. Abuse, rape, torture, it doesn't matter what: the news is, as long as it is not your fault, as long as you are not

*

Every word he says is bullshit, says Alan. It is what I call mathematico-mysticism. Mathematics is not some arcane mumbo-jumbo about the nature of the number one versus the nature of the number two. It is not about the nature of anything at all. Mathematics is an activity, a goal-directed activity, like running.

Since there was no body of law governing relations between groups, it could not be called an offence at law. At the same time it was not quite warfare. It was more like a sport, a cultural activity with serious undertones, like the annual contests, sublimations of battle, played or played out between neighbouring towns in the Europe of yesterday, in which the young men of one town would try to take by force some talismanic object guarded and defended by the young men of another town. (These contests would later be formalized as ball games.)

There are thousands of people from the black areas of South Africa, particularly young men, who get up each morning and, either individually or in bands, set off on raids into the white areas. To them, raiding is their business, their occupation, their recreation, their sport: seeing what they can grab and take back to their homes, preferably without a fight, preferably eluding the professional defenders of property, the police.

Raiding was a nagging thorn in the flesh of the governors of the colony, threatening a cycle of tit-for-tat reprisals that might escalate into warfare. What came to be called apartheid was a new-fangled social-engineering response to a practice that generations of armed farmers had failed to stamp out. After the 1920s, as South Africa's cities began to take on their modern multi-ethnic look,

---

responsible, the dishonour doesn't stick to you. So you have been making yourself miserable over nothing.

Running doesn't have a nature. Running is what you do when you want to get from A to B in a hurry. Mathematics is what you do when you want to get from Q to A, from question to answer, quickly and reliably.

the urban descendants of those farmers were faced with two broad choices in response to raids from black quarters of the cities. One was reactive: to define raiding as a crime and to employ a police force to respond to raids by tracking down and punishing the raiders. The other was proactive: to set up boundaries between black and white areas and police these boundaries, defining each unauthorized intrusion by a black into a white area as an offence in itself.

The reactive option came with a record of failure three centuries long. In 1948 whites voted to take the proactive route, and the rest is history. The institution of boundaries made upward social mobility for blacks, and downward social mobility for whites, near to impossible, congealing class antagonism and race antagonism into a solid mass; while the machinery created to police those boundaries turned into the expensive, tentacular bureaucracy of the apartheid state.

That was it. She had had her say, made her point. My turn to speak.

I wait for more, but that is all.

And probability, I say? What do you think of what he says about probability – that it is all hocus-pocus, and so forth?

21. On apology

In a new book entitled *Sense and Nonsense in Australian History,* John Hirst returns to the question of whether white Australians ought to apologize to Aboriginal Australians for the conquest and takeover of their land. In sceptical spirit he asks whether apology without restitution means anything, whether it is not in fact "nonsense."

This is a burning question not only for the descendants of settlers in Australia but for their equivalents in South Africa too. In South Africa the situation is in one sense better than in Australia: the handover of farmland from white to black, even if it has to be enforced handover, is a practical possibility there as it is not in Australia. The ownership of land, the kind of land that is measured in hectares and on which you can grow crops and run livestock, is of huge symbolic value, even if small-scale farming is declining in importance within the national economy. Every parcel of land transferred from white to black hands thus seems to mark a step in a process of restitutive justice whose end will be the restoration of the status quo ante.

Nothing so dramatic can be projected in Australia, where the pressure from below is, by comparison, slight and intermittent.

No man is an island, I said. She looked blank. We are all part of the main, I said. Things haven't changed, mistress Anya.

More bullshit, says Alan. Ignorant bullshit. He is a hundred years out of date. We live in a probabilistic universe, a quantum universe. Schrödinger proved it. Heisenberg proved it. Einstein disagreed, but he was wrong. He had to admit he was wrong, in the end.

Among non-indigenous Australians all but a small minority hope for the issue to simply go away, in the same way that, in the United States, the issue of indigenous rights to the land was made to go away, to disappear.

In today's newspaper, an advertisement by an American lawyer, an expert on legal liability, who for a fee of $650 an hour will coach Australian companies in how to word apologies without admitting liability. Step by step the formal apology, which used to have the highest symbolic status, becomes devalued as businessmen and politicians learn that in the present climate – what they call the present "culture" – there are ways of taking the moral high ground without risking material loss.

This development is not unconnected with the feminization or sentimentalization of manners that began two or three decades ago. The man who is too stiff to cry or too unbending to apologize – more accurately, who will not perform (convincingly) the act of crying, who will not perform (convincingly) the act of apologizing – has become a dinosaur and a figure of fun, that is to say, has fallen out of fashion.

Dishonour won't be washed away. Won't be wished away.

And before the quantum universe? I say. Before a hundred years ago? Did we live in another kind of universe?

Alan gives me another of his sharp looks, a very sharp one indeed this time, like *I am the boss and don't you forget that*. Whose side are you on, Anya? he says. He never calls me Anya except when he is cross.

I am on your side, Alan, I say. I am always on your side. I just want to hear how the argument goes.

First Adam Smith placed reason in the service of interest; now sentiment is placed in the service of interest too. In the course of this latter development, the concept of sincerity is gutted of all meaning. In the present "culture," few care to distinguish – indeed, few are capable of distinguishing – between sincerity and the performance of sincerity, just as few distinguish between religious faith and religious observance. To the dubious question, Is this true faith? or, Is this true sincerity? one receives only a blank look. Truth? What is that? Sincerity? Of course I'm sincere – didn't I say so?

The expensive American coaches his clients neither in how to perform true (sincere) apologies nor in how to perform false (insincere) apologies that will have the look of true (sincere) apologies, but simply in how to perform apologies that will not open them to being sued. In his eyes and in the eyes of his clients, an unscripted, unrehearsed apology will likely be an excessive, inappropriate, ill-calculated, and therefore false apology, that is to say, one that costs money, money being the measure of all things.

Jonathan Swift, thou shouldst be living at this hour.

Still has its old power to stick. Your three American boys – I have never laid eyes on them, but they dishonour me nevertheless.

It is true, I am on Alan's side. I am with Alan, and being with a man means being on his side. But just recently I have begun to feel crushed between him and Señor C, between hard certainties on the one side and hard opinions on the other, to the point where sometimes I would like to withdraw and go off by myself. If you are so aroused by El Señor's opinions, I want to say to Alan, you be the typist, you type them. Except that he wouldn't bother to type them, he would just tear the tape out of the machine and throw it in the trash. *Bullshit!* he would shout. *Fail! Fail! Fail!* The old bull and the young bull, fighting it out. And me? I am the young cow they are trying to impress, that is getting bored with their antics.

22. On asylum in Australia

I do my best to understand the Australian way of handling refugees, and fail. What baffles me is not the laws themselves that govern petitions for asylum – harsh though they may be, a case can be made for them that is at least plausible – but the way in which they are implemented. How can a decent, generous, easygoing people close their eyes while strangers who arrive on their shores pretty much helpless and penniless are treated with such heartlessness, such grim callousness?

I suppose the answer is that people do not simply close their eyes. I suppose the fact is that they feel uneasy, even sickened, to the point that, in order to save themselves and their sense of being decent, generous, easygoing, etcetera, they have to close their eyes and ears. A natural way of behaving, a human way. Plenty of Third World societies treat lepers with equal heartlessness.

And I would be very surprised if in your inmost depths they did not continue to dishonour you.

He says, says Alan, that if you stand outside probabilistic discourse then probability statements make no sense. That is a fair enough statement as far as it goes. But what he forgets is that in a probabilistic universe *there is nowhere to stand outside probability*. It is all of a piece with his idea that numbers stand for something outside themselves, though he can't say what. The fact is, numbers are just numbers. They don't stand for anything. They are nuts and bolts, the nuts and bolts of mathematics. They are what we utilize when we work with mathematics in the real world. Look around you. Look at bridges. Look at traffic flows. Look at the movement of money. Numbers work. Mathematics works. Probabilities work. That is all we need to know.

As for the people who created the present refugee system and now administer it, it is truly difficult to feel one's way into their state of mind. Do they not have doubts and second thoughts? Perhaps not. If they had meant from the beginning to create a simple, efficient and *human* system of processing refugees, they could surely have done so. What they have created instead is a system of deterrences, and indeed a spectacle of deterrence. It says: *This is the purgatory to which you will be subjected if you arrive in Australia without papers. Think again.* In this respect Baxter Detention Centre out in the South Australian desert is not dissimilar to Guantanamo Bay. *Behold: this is what happens to those who cross the line we have drawn. Be warned.*

As evidence that their system works, the Australian authorities point to the drop in the number of what they call "illegal arrivals" since the system came into operation. And they are right: as a deterrent, their system clearly works. Deterrence, from *terrere*, to terrify.

One forgets that Australia was never a promised land, a new world, an island paradise offering its bounty to the new arrival. It grew out of an archipelago of penal colonies owned by an abstract Crown. First you passed through the entrails of the court system; then you were transported to the ends of the earth. Life in the Antipodes was meant to be a punishment; it made no sense to complain that it was unpleasant.

I had never before thought of Anya as either soft or hard. If I thought of her in a material way at all, it was as sweet: sweet as

---

Have you been spying on me, Alan? I ask quietly.

Alan glares at me. Are you crazy? he says. Why would I want to spy on you?

Today's refugees find themselves in much the same boat as yesterday's transported. Someone, or more likely some committee, concocted a system for "processing" them. That system was approved and adopted, and now it is implemented impersonally, without exceptions, without mercy, even if it dictates that people must be locked up indefinitely in cells in camps in the desert, humiliated and driven mad and then punished for their madness.

As in Guantanamo Bay, the Baxter detention camp (correction: the Baxter *facility*) has among its targets masculine honour, masculine dignity. In the case of Guantanamo Bay it is intended that when prisoners at last emerge from incarceration they will be mere shells of men, psychically wrecked; in the worst cases, Baxter is achieving the same effect.

opposed to salty, gold as opposed to silver, earth as opposed to air. But now suddenly she became quite stone-like, quite flinty.

Alan is good at many things, but not at lying. I see through his lies every time, and he knows it. That is why he glares: to intimidate me, to frighten me off.

I never breathed a single word to you about probability before now, I say. So how come you know what Señor C thinks about probability?

23. On political life in Australia

According to Judith Brett, whose recent disquisition on John Howard's Australia I have been reading, the Australian Liberal Party, like Margaret Thatcher, does not believe in the existence of society. That is to say, it has an empirical ontology which declares that, unless you can kick something, it does not exist. Society, in its eyes as in Thatcher's, is an abstraction invented by academic sociologists.[7]

What the Liberals do believe to exist are (a) the individual, (b) the family, and (c) the nation. Family and nation are the two objectively existent (in the sense of being kickable) groupings into which individuals fall. To nation and to family the individual ineluctably, by birth, belongs. Every other grouping between the level of family and the level of nation has a voluntary character: as one may choose which football club to join, or indeed choose not to join a football club at all, so one may choose one's religion and even one's class.

From her eyes beamed a ray of pure cold rage. *Don't you tell me how I feel!* she hissed. She was too slight of figure to be regal, too inappropriately clad too, but she drew herself up to her fullest queenly height. *What do you know!*

I have never spied on you, Alan blusters. I would never do such a thing. But, since you ask, I will tell you how I come to know. There is a reporting program on the computer in his flat. It reports back to me on what he is up to.

For a moment I am so flabbergasted that I cannot speak. But why would you do that? I say at last. He doesn't use a computer anyway, his eyesight is too bad. I thought I told you. That is why he hired me.

There may seem to be something naïve and even blinkered in Howard's belief that, simply by dint of hard work and saving, one can leave one's origins behind and join the great Australian no-class. On the other hand, what Howard sees as uniquely – and definingly – Australian is precisely a widespread goodwill that encourages people to rise above the circumstances into which they were born. (Here the contrast he would see is with the mother country, Great Britain, where subtle bonds tie one into the class of one's birth.) And the good luck of prosperous times would seem to confirm Howard's view: a goodly proportion of today's middle-class Australians – middle-class by the economistic criteria which are all that count to the Liberals – come from working-class backgrounds.

The limitations of this simplistic attitude to society emerge in matters of race and culture. A non-racist Australia is, in Liberal eyes, a land in which there are no barriers to prevent a person of Aboriginal or any other racial descent from becoming a full member in the Australian nation and a full participant ("player") in the Australian economy. All that is needed to achieve full Australian status is energy, hard work, and a belief in one's (individual) self.

The next morning, along with the computer disk, there was a note in my letterbox in her plump, rather schoolgirlish hand:

Well, he does use the computer. I know that for a fact. He uses it every day. He uses it for e-mail. All the stuff you do for him goes onto his hard drive. That is where I came across it. If he told you his eyesight is too bad to type, it is a fib. What he has lost is fine muscular control. That is why he is so slow on the keyboard.

A similar naïve optimism reigned among well-meaning whites in South Africa after 1990, when job-reservation legislation based on race was scrapped. To these folk, the end of apartheid meant that there would no longer be barriers to individuals, no matter what their race, realizing their full economic potential. Hence their bafflement when the African National Congress brought in legislation that privileged blacks on the job market. To liberals there could be no step more retrogressive, a step back into the old days when the colour of one's skin counted for more than education or aspirations or diligence.

Liberals, in Australia as in South Africa, feel that it should be left to the market to decide who shall rise and who shall not. The role of government should be self-limited: to create conditions in which individuals can bring their aspirations, their drive, their training, and whatever other forms of intangible capital they have, to the market, which will then (here comes the moment when economic philosophy turns into religious faith) reward them more or less in proportion to their contribution (their "input").

Though I was born in earlier times, I was brought up in essentially the same school of thought, with its suspicion of philosophical idealism and of ideas in general, its dog-eat-dog individualism, its narrow conception of self-advancement, and its ethics of hard work.

This is the last typing I can do for you. I cannot stand your undermining of me. A.

That is why his handwriting looks like a child's. That is why he hired you. To do his typing for him. But that was never the main reason. He is obsessed with you, Anya. I don't know if you realize it. Don't get angry with me. I am not jealous. It's a free country. What he chooses to obsess about is his business. But you ought to know.

All that was lacking in my day was an optimistic faith in the market. The market, I learned from my mother, was a dark and sinister machine that ground down and ate up a hundred destinies for every lucky individual it rewarded. My mother's generation had a distinctly pre-modern attitude to the market: it was a creation of the devil; only the wicked prospered in the market. For hard work there was no certain reward on this earth; nevertheless, without hard work there would be no reward at all, except of course in the case of the wicked, the "crooks." It was a cast of mind reinforced by the novelists they favoured: Hardy, Galsworthy, the tragic naturalists.

Hence the stupid doggedness with which I pursue my little projects, even today. Stubbornly I believe that labour is in itself good, whether or not it achieves measurable results. Looking over the record of my life, an economic rationalist would smile and shake his head.

"We are all players in the global market: if we do not compete, we will perish." The market is where we are, where we find ourselves. How we got to be here we may not ask. It is like being born into a world we have no hand in choosing, to parents unknown. We are here, that is all. Now it is our fate to compete.

I propped the note on the table before me. How should I read it?

What else have you been spying on, Alan, that you haven't told me?

He is silent.

To true believers in the market, it makes no sense to say that you take no pleasure in competing with your fellow men and prefer to withdraw. You may withdraw if you wish, they say, but your competitors will most assuredly not. As soon as you lay down your arms, you will be slaughtered. We are locked ineluctably into a battle of all against all.

But surely God did not make the market – God or the Spirit of History. And if we human beings made it, can we not unmake it and remake it in a kindlier form? Why does the world have to be a kill-or-be-killed gladiatorial amphitheatre rather than, say, a busily collaborative beehive or anthill?

In favour of the arts it can at least be said that, while every artist strives for the best, attempts to cast the sphere of the arts as a competitive jungle have had little success. Business likes to finance competitions in the arts, as it is even readier to pour money into competitive sport. But, unlike sportspeople, artists know that the competition is not the real thing, is only a publicity sideshow. The eyes of the artist are, finally, not on the competition but on the true, the good, and the beautiful.

As a notice of termination of contract from my typist, and nothing more? As a cry for help from a young woman more troubled of soul than I had dreamed?

Are you saying that he writes about me in secret? Have you been reading his private diary? Because, if you have, that will really make me angry. What a mess! What a mess! I wish I had never got involved. But tell me the truth: Are you poking around among his private thoughts?

(Interesting how the march of mercenary individualism drives one into the corner of reactionary idealism.)

What of the Australian Labor Party? Having suffered one electoral defeat after another, the ALP is now criticized for recruiting its leadership from within too narrow a political caste, from people with no experience of life outside politics and outside the party. I have no doubt that the criticism is just. But the ALP is by no means unique. It is an elementary fallacy to conclude that because in a democracy politicians represent the people therefore politicians are representative people. The closed-off life of the typical politician is much like life in a military caste or in the Mafia or in Kurosawa's bandit gangs. One commences one's career at the bottom of the ladder, running errands and spying; when one has proved one's loyalty and obedience and readiness to endure ritual humiliations, one is blooded into the gang proper; thereafter one's first duty is to the gang leader.

Dear Anya, I wrote:

I couldn't care a rat's arse about his private thoughts. It is other things I am interested in.

Like what?

Alan squirms like a little boy, but his embarrassment doesn't run deep. I know what sort of childhood he had: lonely, unsure, desperate to be noticed. From the moment he met me he has been demanding praise and attention. It is as if I have taken the place of his mother. Now he is bursting to share his new secret.

24. On Left and Right

Next week there will be federal elections in Canada, and the Conservatives are tipped to win. I am flummoxed by the drift to the Right in the countries of the West. Electorates have the spectacle before them, in the United States, of where the Right will take them if given half a chance, yet they vote Right anyway.

The bogeyman Osama bin Laden has succeeded beyond his wildest dreams. Armed with nothing but Kalashnikovs and plastic explosives, he and his followers have terrorized and demoralized the West, driving nations into wholesale panic. To the bullying, authoritarian, militaristic strand in Western political life, Osama has been a gift from the gods.

In Australia and Canada electorates behave like frightened sheep.

You have become indispensable to me – to me and to the present project. I cannot imagine handing over the manuscript to someone else. It would be like taking a child away from its natural mother and putting it in a stranger's care.

Like his finances, he says. I told you. Like what is going to happen with his assets after he dies. He is an incompetent, Anya, a financial incompetent. He has three million dollars plus – *three million!* – sitting in savings accounts drawing four and a half per cent interest. Less tax that is two and a half per cent. So in real terms he is actually *losing* money every day. And do you know what will happen to that three million when he dies? He has a will, dating back to September 1990, unrevised, in terms of which all his assets – the money, the flat and its contents, plus intangible assets like copyrights – go to his sister. *But his sister has been dead for seven years.* I checked on that. And the secondary heir is a charity, some dead-end organization where his sister used to work, that rehabilitates laboratory animals.

South Africa, where Islamist extremism still takes a lowly place on the list of public concerns, begins to look like a sensible elder brother. What an irony!

What I liked best about Australia, when I first visited in the 1990s, was the way in which people conducted themselves in their everyday dealings: frankly, fairly, with an elusive personal pride and an equally elusive ironic reserve. Now, fifteen years later, I hear the sense of self embodied in that conduct disparaged in many quarters as belonging to an Australia of a past now outmoded. As the material foundations of "old" social relations erode before my eyes, these relations take on the status of manners rather than of living cultural reflexes. Australian society may never – thank God! – become quite as selfish and cruel as American society, but it does seem to be sleepwalking in that direction.

Strange to find oneself missing what one has never had, has never even been part of. Strange to find oneself feeling elegiac about a past one never really knew.

In his recently published history of post-1945 Europe, Tony Judt suggests that in the twenty-first century Europe may replace the United States as the model to which the rest of the world will look

---

I urge you, please reconsider.

Laboratory animals?

Animals that have been used in laboratory experiments. So in effect the money goes to animals. All of it. And that is his will, period! As I say, never revised. His last wishes, in the eyes of the law.

You have seen this will?

up for material prosperity, enlightened social policies, and personal freedom. But how strong is the commitment to personal freedom among Europe's political class? There is evidence that some of Europe's security agencies are collaborating or colluding with the CIA to the point where in effect they report to Washington. In eastern Europe some of the governments seem to be in the pocket of the US. We may expect the state of affairs that prevails in the United Kingdom of Tony Blair to spread: anti-American feeling among the populace, but a government that dances to the American tune. We may even, in due course, see reproduced over part of Europe what existed in eastern Europe in the days of the USSR: a bloc of national states whose governments are, by some definition of democracy, democratically elected, but key areas of whose policies are dictated by a foreign power, where dissent is gagged and popular manifestations against the foreign power are suppressed by force.

The one bright spot in a dismal picture is provided by Latin America, with the unexpected coming to power of a handful of socialist-populist governments. Alarm bells must be ringing in Washington: we can expect rising levels of diplomatic coercion, economic warfare, and downright subversion.

Yours,
JC

I have seen everything. Will, back correspondence with his solicitor, bank accounts, passwords. As I said, I have a reporting programme. It reports. That is what it is there for.

You have installed spyware on his computer?

Interesting that at the moment in history when neo-liberalism proclaims that, politics having at last been subsumed under economics, the old categories of Left and Right have become obsolete, people all over the world who had been content to think of themselves as "moderate" – that is, as opposed to the excesses of both Left and Right – should be deciding that in an age of Right triumphalism the idea of a Left is too precious to abandon.

In the orthodox, neo-liberal view, socialism collapsed and died under its own contradictions. But might we not entertain an alternative story: that socialism did not collapse but was bludgeoned to the ground, did not die but was killed?

We think of the Cold War as a period when real war, hot war, was held at bay while two rival economic systems, capitalist and socialist, competed to see who could win the hearts and minds of the peoples of the world. But would the hundreds of thousands of men and women of the idealist Left, perhaps millions, who were imprisoned and tortured and executed during those years for their political beliefs and public actions concur with that account of the times? Was there not a hot war going on all the time during the cold war, a war waged in cellars and prison cells and interrogation rooms around the world, into whose conduct billions of dollars were poured, until it was finally won, until the battered ship of socialist idealism gave up and sank?

Was it true? Was Anya from 2514 in any but the most far-fetched sense the natural mother of the miscellany of opinions I was putting down on paper on commission from Mittwoch Verlag of Herderstrasse, Berlin? No. The passions and prejudices out of

---

I told you. I have got a little software package encoded on his hard drive inside what looks like a photograph. It is completely invisible unless you know what you are hunting for. No one will pick it up. And I can erase it from the outside if I want to.

But what has this to do with you? Why are you interested in his will?

25. On Tony Blair

The story of Tony Blair could come straight out of Tacitus. An ordinary little middle-class boy with all the correct attitudes (the rich should subsidize the poor, the military should be kept on a tight rein, civil rights should be defended against the inroads of the state), but with no philosophical grounding and little capacity for introspection, and with no inner compass save personal ambition, embarks on the voyage of politics, with all its warping forces, and ends up an enthusiast for entrepreneurial greed and the sedulous monkey of masters in Washington, turning a dutifully blind eye (see no evil, hear no evil) while their shadowy agents assassinate, torture and "disappear" opponents at will.

In private moments men like Blair defend themselves by saying that their critics (always labelled armchair critics) forget that in this less than ideal world politics is the art of the possible. They go further: politics is not for sissies, they say, by sissies meaning people reluctant to compromise moral principles. By nature politics is uncongenial to the truth, they say, or at least to the practice of telling the truth under all circumstances. History will vindicate them, they conclude by saying – history with its longer view.

which my opinions grew were laid down long before I first set eyes on Anya, and were by now so strong – that is to say, so settled, so rigid – that aside from the odd word here and there there was no chance that refraction through her gaze could alter their angle.

Let me ask you a question, Anya. Who can make better use of three million dollars: a bunch of rats and cats and dogs and monkeys that have already had their brains scrambled in scientific experiments and should be thankful to be put down humanely; or you and me?

There have been occasions when people who have come to power have sworn to themselves to practise a politics of truth, or at least a politics that eschews the lie. Fidel Castro may once have been such a person. But how brief is the time before the exigencies of political life make it difficult and eventually impossible for the man in power to tell the difference between the truth and the lie!

Like Blair, Fidel will in private say, *It is all very well to deliver your lofty judgment, but you do not know what pressures I was under.* Always it is the so-called reality principle such people adduce; always criticism of them is spurned as idealistic, unrealistic.

What ordinary people grow tired of hearing from their rulers are declarations that are never quite the truth: a little short of the truth, or else a little beside the truth, or else the truth with a spin to it that makes it wobble. They long for relief from incessant prevarication. Hence their hunger (a mild hunger, it must be admitted) to hear what articulate people from outside the political world – academics or churchmen or scientists or writers – think about public affairs.

But how can this hunger be satisfied by the mere writer (to speak just of writers) when the grasp of the facts that the writer has is usually incomplete or unsure, when his very access to the so-called facts is likely to be via media within the political field of forces, and when, half the time, he is because of his vocation as much interested in the liar and the psychology of the lie as in the truth?

Opiniâtre, say the French: obdurate, stony, mulish. Bruno, in his German, is more diplomatic. He is still wavering between

---

You and me?

That's right: you and me.

I don't mean you and me, I mean, what has his money to do with you and me?

26. On Harold Pinter

Harold Pinter, winner of the 2005 Nobel Prize for literature, is too ill to travel to Stockholm for the ceremony. But in a recorded lecture he makes what can fairly be called a savage attack on Tony Blair for his part in the war in Iraq, calling for him to be put on trial as a war criminal.

When one speaks in one's own person – that is, not through one's art – to denounce some politician or other, using the rhetoric of the agora, one embarks on a contest which one is likely to lose because it takes place on ground where one's opponent is far more practised and adept. "Of course Mr Pinter is entitled to his point of view," it will be replied. "After all, he enjoys the freedoms of a democratic society, freedoms which we are this moment endeavouring to protect against extremists."

So it takes some gumption to speak as Pinter has spoken. Who knows, perhaps Pinter sees quite clearly that he will be slickly refuted, disparaged, even ridiculed. Despite which he fires the first shot and steels himself for the reply. What he has done may be foolhardy but it is not cowardly. And there come times when the outrage and the shame are so great that all calculation, all prudence, is overwhelmed and one must act, that is to say, speak.

---

calling these little excursions *Meinungen* or *Ansichten*. *Meinungen* are opinions, he says, but opinions subject to fluctuations of mood.

I am going to put that money to some use, Anya. Make it work for a change, instead of dozing in a bank account. On three million I can get fourteen or fifteen per cent, easily. We make fifteen per cent, we give him back his five per cent, we take the rest as commission, as the fruits of intellectual labour. That is three hundred thousand per annum. If he lives another three years it is a million. And he won't even know about it. As far as he is concerned, interest will go on accruing every quarter.

27. On music

In doctors' waiting-rooms, a decade or two ago, the tedium would have been relieved with quiet background music: sentimental songs from Broadway, popular classics like Vivaldi's *Four Seasons*. Nowadays, however, one hears only the thudding, mechanical music favoured by the young. Their cowed elders bear it without protest: *faute de mieux* it has become their music too.

The rupture is not likely to be repaired. The bad drives out the good: what they call "classical" music is simply no longer cultural currency. Is there anything of interest to be said of the development, or must one just grouse about it under one's breath?

The *Meinungen* I held yesterday are not necessarily the *Meinungen* I hold today. *Ansichten*, by contrast, are firmer, more thought out.

You have left me behind. How can he not know about it when funds suddenly disappear out of his bank account and go into the stock market?

Because all his bank statements, all his electronic communications will come through me. They will be diverted. Make a detour. I will fix them. For the duration.

Music expresses feeling, that is to say, gives shape and habitation to feeling, not in space but in time. To the extent that music has a history that is more than a history of its formal evolution, our feelings must have a history too. Perhaps certain qualities of feeling that found expression in music in the past, and were recorded to the extent that music can be recorded by being notated on paper, have become so remote that we can no longer inhabit them as feelings, can get a grasp of them only after long training in the history and philosophy of music, the philosophical history of music, the history of music as a history of the feeling soul.

From such a premise one might go on to identify qualities of feeling that have not survived into the twenty-first century of Our Lord. A good place to start would be the music of the nineteenth century, since there are some of us around to whom the inner life of nineteenth-century man is not quite dead, not yet.

In our last communication he was tending to prefer *Meinungen.*

You are crazy! If his accountant gets suspicious, or if he dies and the estate goes to the lawyers, the trail will lead straight to you. You will go to jail. It will be the end of your career.

Consider singing. Nineteenth-century art-song is very remote in its kinaesthetics from singing today. The nineteenth-century singer was trained to sing from the depths of her thorax (from her lungs, from her "heart"), bearing the head high, emitting a large, rounded tone of the kind that carries. It is a mode of singing meant to convey moral nobility. In performances that were of course always live, those present had staged before their eyes the contrast between the mere physical body and the voice that transcends the body, emerging from it, rising above it, and leaving it behind.

From the body, thus, song was born as soul. And that birth took place not without pain, not without pangs: the link between feeling and pain was emphasized in such words as *passio*, *Leidenschaft*. The very sound that the singer produced – rounded, echoing – had a reflective quality.

*

Six different writers, six different personalities, he says: how can we be sure how firmly wedded each writer is to his opinions?

The trail won't lead to me. On the contrary, the trail will lead to a foundation in Switzerland that manages a group of neurology clinics and gives grants to researchers into Parkinsonism; and if they want to follow the trail further than that it will take them from Zurich to a holding company registered in the Cayman Islands; at which point they will be forced to give up, since we have no treaty with the Caymans. I will be completely invisible, from beginning to end. Like God. And so will you.

What Cartesian nonsense to think of birdsong as pre-programmed cries uttered by birds to advertise their presence to the opposite sex, and so forth! Each bird-cry is a full-hearted release of the self into the air, accompanied by such joy as we can barely comprehend. *I!* says each cry: *I! What a miracle!* Singing liberates the voice, allows it to fly, expands the soul. In the course of a military training, on the other hand, people are drilled in using the voice in a rapid, flat, mechanical manner, without pause for thought. What damage it must do to the soul to submit to the military voice, to embody it as one's own!

I recall an episode that took place years ago in the library of Johns Hopkins University in Baltimore. I made some or other enquiry of a librarian, from whom each question of mine elicited a swift, monotone response, leaving me with the unsettling feeling that I was speaking not to a fellow human being but to a machine. Indeed, the young woman seemed to take pride in her machine identity, in its self-sufficiency. There was nothing she sought from me in the exchange, nothing I could give her, not even the salving moment of mutual recognition that two ants give each other as they brush antennae in passing.

Best to leave the question open. What interests the reader more, anyhow, is the quality of the opinions themselves – their variety,

---

Switzerland? Parkinsonism? You mean Parkinson's disease?

Parkinson's disease. That is what he is so worried about, your man Señor C. That is why he needs a young secretary with nimble fingers. That is why he is in such a rush to get his book finished. His opinions. His farewell to the world. So, as regards the hitches you mention, even if he decides to pop off early, his accounts will be in perfect order. The records will show that his money went as a philanthropic donation to medical research. I have constructed a whole e-mail correspondence, dating back over years, between himself and the administrators of the Swiss foundation, ready to be lodged in his computer at a moment's notice.

Much of the ugliness of the speech one hears in the streets of America comes from hostility to song, from repression of the impulse to sing, circumscription of the soul. In the education of the young in America, instead, the inculcation of mechanical, military patterns of speech. Inculcate, from *calx/calcis*, the heel. To inculcate: to tread in.

One can of course hear stunted and mechanical speech all over the world. But pride in the mechanical mode seems to be uniquely American. For in America the model of the self as a ghost inhabiting a machine goes almost unquestioned at a popular level. The body as conceived in America, the American body, is a complex machine comprising a vocal module, a sexual module, and several more, even a psychological module. Inside the body-machine the ghostly self checks read-outs and taps keys, giving commands which the body obeys.

---

their power to startle, the ways in which they match or do not match the reputations of their authors.

And how did you get this spyware of yours onto his computer? It was on one of the disks you gave him. So you used me.

Athletes all over the world have absorbed the American model of self and body, presumably because of the influence of American sports psychology (which "gives results"). Athletes speak openly of themselves as machines of a biological variety that have to be fed certain nutrients in certain quantities at certain times of the day, and "worked" in various ways by their taskmasters to be brought to optimum performance level.

One imagines the lovemaking of such athletes: vigorous activity, followed by a burst of orgasm, rationalized as a kind of reward to the physical mechanism, followed by a brief winding-down period during which the ghostly supervisor confirms that performance has been up to standard.

*

Old people still querulously demand to know why music cannot continue in the tradition of the great nineteenth-century symphonists. The answer is simple. The animating principles of that music are dead and cannot be revived. One cannot compose a nineteenth-century symphony that will not be an instant museum piece.

I disagree. *Ansichten* is the word I want, I say, *Harte Ansichten*, if you can say that in German. *Feste Ansichten*, says Bruno.

If I hadn't used you I would have found another way. This is not a game, Anya. We are talking about a serious amount of money. Not *ultimo* serious, but serious nevertheless. And, before I stepped in, it was being seriously wasted.

Brahms, Tchaikovsky, Bruckner, Mahler, Elgar, Sibelius composed within the bounds of symphonic form a music of heroic rebirth and/or transfiguration. Wagner and Strauss did much the same in forms of their own invention. Theirs is music that relies on parallels between harmonic and motival transmutation on the one hand and spiritual transfiguration on the other. Typically, the progression is through murky struggle toward clarification – hence the note of triumph on which so much of the symphonic music of the period ends.

Curious, given how alien the ideal of spiritual transformation has become, that the music of transformation still retains some of its power to move us, to create a swelling feeling of exaltation, such an odd emotion in our day.

More difficult to pin down are the animating principles of the music of our own times. But certainly we can say that the quality of yearning, of erotic idealism, so common in earlier Romantic music has vanished, probably for good, as have heroic struggle and the striving toward transcendence.

Let me give it further thought. Let me consult with the other contributors.

Not a game, says Alan. I could not agree more. A serious amount. The real thing. Alan has never hid it from me that he does not believe in black and white. It is all a continuum, says Alan, all shades of grey, from darker shades at one end to lighter shades at the other. And he? He is a specialist in the middle area, that is how he puts it, in the shades of grey that are neither dark nor light. But in Señor C's case he seems to me to be crossing the line from grey into black, into the out-and-out blackest.

In the popular music of the twentieth century there has been a newfound rootedness in body-experience. Looking back from the twenty-first century, we see with surprise how rhythmically bare a notion of dance sufficed, first for the aristocratic courts of Europe, then later for the European middle class. The court dances of Rameau, Bach, Mozart, to say nothing of Beethoven, sound quite leaden-footed by today's standard. Even by the late eighteenth century musicians were becoming restive about this state of affairs, looking around for more rhythmically challenging dances to import. Again and again they dip into the music of Europe's peasantry, of gypsies, of the Balkans and Turkey and Central Asia, to refresh the rhythms of European high music. The culmination of this practice is the ostentatious primitivism of Stravinsky's *Rite of Spring.*

What has begun to change since I moved into the orbit of Anya is not my opinions themselves so much as my opinion of my opinions. As I read through what mere hours before she translated from a record of my speaking voice into 14-point type, there are flickering moments when I can see these hard opinions of mine

---

Have you thought this through properly, Alan? I say. Have you thought it through, and are you sure you want to proceed? . Because, frankly, I'm not sure I am with you.

But the really great refreshing of popular music takes place in the New World, via the music of slaves who have not lost their African roots. From North and South America, African rhythms spread over all of the West. It would not be too much to say that through African music Westerners begin to live in and through their bodies in a new way. The colonizers end up being colonized. Even so rhythmically nimble a fellow as Bach would feel out of place, as if on a different continent, were he to be reborn today.

Romantic music seeks to recover a lost state of raptness (which is not the same as rapture), a state of exaltation in which the human shell will be shed and one will become pure being or pure spirit. Hence the continual *striving* in Romantic music: it is always trying to push further (is there not a piece by Mendelssohn called "On Wings of Song" – the earthbound poet yearning to take flight?).

---

through her eyes – see how alien and antiquated they may seem to a thoroughly modern Millie, like the bones of some odd extinct creature, half bird, half reptile, on the point of turning into stone.

I am not asking you to be with me, my sweet. I can bring it off perfectly well by myself. If you don't like what I am doing, then just forget this conversation ever took place. Continue as before. Do his typing. Chat to him. Be nice. Be friendly. I will take care of the rest.

One begins to understand the basis of the Romantic enthusiasm for Bach. Characteristically, Bach shows how in almost any musical germ, no matter how simple, there lie endless possibilities for development. The contrast with more popular composers of his day is marked: in Telemann, for instance, a piece of music sounds like the application of a template rather than the exploration of a potential.

Is it too much to say that the music we call Romantic has an erotic inspiration – that it unceasingly pushes further, tries to enable the listening subject to leave the body behind, to be rapt away (as if harking to birdsong, heavensong), to become a living soul? If this is true, then the erotics of Romantic music could not be more different from the erotics of the present day. In young lovers today one detects not the faintest flicker of that old metaphysical hunger, whose code word for itself was yearning (*Sehnsucht*).

Laments. Fulminations. Curses.

Forget this conversation. Three hundred thousand a year, presumably undeclared, trickling into some or other bank account of Alan's. And when the old man dies, his money magically reappears in his own bank account, all of it, the real money, the real numbers, not the fictions Alan will be feeding him from unit 2514 upstairs; while at the same time the foundation, the mythical Swiss foundation, retreats into the Alpine mists.

28. On tourism

In 1904, at the age of nineteen, Ezra Pound enrolled in a course in Provençal at Hamilton College in the state of New York. From Hamilton he went on to the University of Pennsylvania to pursue his linguistic studies. His ambition was to become a scholar of Romance literatures, and specifically of the poetry of the late Middle Ages.

As a field of study, Provençal literature was more fashionable a hundred years ago than it is today. People of a secular-humanist bent traced the spirit of civilization, modern Western civilization, first back to Greece, then forward again to twelfth-century France and thirteenth-century Italy. Athens defined civilization; Provence and the Quattrocento rediscovered Athens. In Pound's eyes, Provence marked one of the rare moments when life and art and the religious impulse cohered to bring civilization to a point of rich flowering, before the papal persecutions ushered in the old darkness.

I should have heard her out on the subject of honour, let her have the rhetorical victory she was after. I could still do so: go upstairs, knock on her door, say: *You are right, I concede, honour has lost its power, dishonour is dead, now come back to me.*

It is crookery, no doubt about that. It is also, in a certain sense, and on condition that the stock market behaves predictably, that is to say, according to the laws of probability, harmless. So am I being given a glimpse of how Alan spends his days: performing crooked but (hopefully) harmless tricks with other people's money? Am I sharing my life with a professional swindler?

In 1908 Pound sailed for the first time to Europe, where he busied himself in literary affairs while proceeding with his Romance explorations. In 1912 he embarked on a tour in the footsteps of his troubadour heroes. The first part of the tour took in Poitiers, Angoulême, Périgueux, and Limoges. The second led from Uzerche to Souillac, then to Sarlat, Cahors, Rodez, Albi, and Toulouse. From Toulouse he proceeded to Foix, Lavelanet, Quillan, and Carcassonne, and thence to Béziers.

His plan was to use the tour as material for a travel cum cultural history book to be entitled *Gironde*. However, the publisher to whom he was contracted went out of business, and the book was never written. All that survives are some notebooks, now in the Yale collection, from which Richard Sieburth has transcribed and published excerpts.

And perhaps – who knows? – it would be not wholly a lie. Perhaps what I feel descending upon me when I am confronted with images, recorded with zoom lenses from far away, of men in orange suits, shackled and hooded, shuffling about like zombies behind the barbed wire of Guantanamo Bay, is not really the

---

Are the police going to knock on the door one morning and drag Alan off with his jacket pulled over his head; and are there going to be photographers camped across the road waiting to snap a picture of the girlfriend of the accused?

Pound seems to have believed that he could not properly appreciate troubadour poetry until he had travelled the roads and seen the landscapes familiar to his poets. On the face of it, this seems reasonable. The trouble is that in troubadour poetry the specifics of landscape do not figure. We do indeed encounter birds and flowers, but they are generic birds, generic flowers. We know what the troubadours must have seen, but we do not know what they saw.

A decade ago, following in the tracks of Pound and his poets, I cycled some of those same roads, in particular (several times) the road between Foix and Lavelanet past Roquefixade. What I achieved by doing so I am not sure. I am not even sure what my illustrious predecessor expected to achieve. Both of us set out on the basis that writers who were important to us (to Pound, the troubadours; to me, Pound) had actually been where we were, in flesh and blood; but neither of us seemed or seem able to demonstrate in our writing why or how that mattered.

dishonour, the disgrace of being alive in these times, but something else, something punier and more manageable, some overload or underload of amines in the cortex that could loosely be entitled *depression* or even more loosely *gloom* and could be dispelled in a matter of minutes by the right cocktail of chemicals X, Y and Z.

It is just cats and dogs, Anya, he says, circling me, coming up behind me, putting his arms around me, speaking softly into my ear. If the worst comes to the worst, it is just cats and dogs with sensors and drips and lengths of wire hanging out of them. Where is the actual harm? In the worst scenario, if there is some hitch we haven't foreseen, we will simply close down and everything will go back to being as it was before.

To me, all that was extraordinary about seeing Roquefixade for the first time was to find how ordinary Roquefixade was: just another point on the great globe. It gave me no shivers. I detect no sign that it gave Pound shivers either. The sights from the 1912 tour that made an impression on him, that stayed in his memory and found their way into his poetry, are quite arbitrary: a stile announcing a path that led nowhere, for example (see the fragments that conclude the *Cantos*).

The nature of tourism has changed since 1912. The idea of following in the footsteps of X or Y has dwindled as historical events have become confused with re-enactments of historical events, old ("historical") objects with simulacra of old objects (Viollet-le-Duc rebuilding the walls of Carcassonne). Cycling the roads of the Languedoc, I was probably the only person in a radius of a hundred miles who was in any sense paying homage to the great dead.

I should thoroughly revise my opinions, that is what I should do.

The worst scenario is a lot worse than that, Alan. As you could see for yourself if you would just pause to think.

I have paused and thought. I have thought long and hard. I don't foresee what could happen that would be worse than the worst I have planned for. Enlighten me.

29. On English usage

A while ago I began compiling a list of modish usages in present-day English. At the head of the list were the antonymic pair *appropriate/inappropriate*, the phrase *going forward*, and the ubiquitous compound preposition *in terms of.*

Inappropriate, I noted, has come to replace *bad* or *wrong* in the speech of people who wish to express disapproval without seeming to express a moral judgment (to such people, moral judgment in itself is to be shunned as inappropriate). Thus: "She testified that the stranger had touched her inappropriately."

As for *going forward*, which supplants *in future* or *in the future*, it is used to suggest that the speaker faces the future full of optimism and energy. "Despite this quarter's lacklustre numbers, we expect a rapid expansion going forward."

I should cull the older, more decrepit ones, find newer, up-to-date ones to replace them. But where does one go to find up-to-date opinions? To Anya? To her lover and moral guide, the broker-man Alan? Can one buy fresh opinions in the marketplace?

I could begin to look at you in a different way. Have you thought about that? Alan, I am formally serving you notice: if you push ahead with this scheme of yours, things will never be the same between us.

Less easy to account for is the all-purpose preposition *in terms of:* "They made a lot of money *in terms of* (instead of *in*) bribes"; "They made a lot of money *in terms of* (instead of *through*) graft"; "They made a lot of money *in terms of* (instead of *under*) false pretences"; "They made a lot of money *in terms of* (instead of *with*) intelligent investments"; "They made a lot of money *in terms of* (instead of *by*) investing intelligently".

The rationale seems to run as follows. The underlying logical form of the declarative sentence is propositional, that is to say, the sentence can be broken down into a subject plus a predicate that makes an assertion about the subject. The predicate may have a number of arguments linked to it. These arguments may or may not take the form of prepositional phrases. In the case of prepositional phrases, the specific preposition at the head of the phrase (in the phrase *in bribes*, the preposition *in*) is more or less dictated by the combined semantic content of the verb (*make money*) and the rest of the prepositional phrase (*bribes*). The preposition itself thus carries little informational load; it may as well be semantically null.

Are old men with doddering intellect and poor eyesight and arthritic hands allowed on the trading floor, or will we just get in the way of the young?

We have never fought, Alan and I, not seriously. We are a level-headed couple. Because we are level-headed, because we don't have unreasonable expectations, because we don't make unreasonable demands, we have a successful relationship. We have been around the block, both of us, we know the score.

On the basis of such reasoning, one can argue that there is in fact little call for a range of prepositions, each with its own meaning: all we need is a single all-purpose marker to announce the start of a prepositional phrase. *In terms of* fulfils this function.

The merging of the old repertoire of prepositions into a single one suggests that an as yet unarticulated decision has been made by an influential body of English speakers: that the degree of specificity demanded by approved English usage is unnecessary for the strict purposes of communication, and therefore that a degree of simplification is in order.

We see a comparable development in the simplification of the rule of concord between subject and verb: "Fear of terrorist attacks are affecting travel plans." The emerging new rule of concord seems to be that the number of the verb is determined not by its subject but by the number of the noun most closely preceding it. We may be on the road to a grammar (an internalized grammar) in which the notion *grammatical subject of* is not present.

PS, I wrote. Some news. I am beginning to put together a second, gentler set of opinions. I will be happy to show them to you if that will persuade you to return. Some of them take up suggestions that you let drop. A gentle opinion on birds, for example. A gentle opinion on love, or at least on kissing between a gentleman and a lady. Can I induce you to take a look?

I give him space, he gives me space. I don't step on his toes, he doesn't step on mine. So what is happening to us now? Have we slipped, willy-nilly, into our first big fight?

My notes on these developments in linguistic usage grew in length, to the point where they began to turn into an essay. But what sort of essay was I engaged in: a piece of objective linguistic analysis or a veiled diatribe on declining standards? Could I maintain a tone of scholarly detachment, or would I ineluctably be taken over by the spirit in which Flaubert wrote his *Dictionary of Received Ideas*, a spirit of impotent scorn? Whatever the case, would an essay published in one or other Australian journal have any more effect on everyday English speech than Flaubert's loftily disdainful notes had on habits of thought among the bourgeoisie of his day? Can the argument really be sustained – an argument dear to the hearts of prescriptivist teachers – that muddle in action can be traced to muddled thought, and muddled thought to muddled language? Most scientists can't write for toffee, yet in their professional life who practises exact thinking better than they? Might the uncomfortable truth (uncomfortable for people who have an investment in

It took a whole day of waiting – a day during which I fretted so

It is as if Alan reads what I am thinking. Is this a fight, Anya? he says. Because if it is, it is not worth it. I will give up the plan, I promise, if you really want me to. Just cool down. Sleep on it. Reflect. Tell me tomorrow what you decide. But bear in mind: it is just dogs and cats. And rats. It is the Anti-Vivisection League of Australia. That is its name. Not UNESCO. Not Oxfam.

linguistic correctness) not be that ordinary people use language as exactly as they feel to be required by the circumstances, that the test they use is whether their interlocutor gets their meaning, that in most cases an interlocutor who shares their language (their social and professional dialect) can quickly and easily and successfully work out their meaning (which is seldom complex anyway), and therefore that lapses of concord or bizarreries of syntax ("The fact is, is that . . .") make no practical difference? As ordinary speakers so often say when the words begin to get away from them: "You know what I mean."

I survey my elderly coevals and see all too many consumed with grouchiness, all too many who allow their helpless bafflement about the way things are going to turn into the main theme of their final years. We will not be like that, we vow, each of us: we will heed the lesson of old King Knut, we will retreat gracefully before the tide of the times. But, truly, sometimes it is difficult.

---

much that I wrote not a word – but it worked. The doorbell rang.

It is a couple of old women in a one-room office in Surry Hills with a desk and a Remington typewriter and a box of dusty old pamphlets and a cage in the corner full of rats with wires in their heads. That is who you are choosing to fight for, against me. That is who you want to save. Three million dollars. They wouldn't have the first idea what to do with it. If they even exist any more. If they haven't gone under.

30. On authority in fiction

In the novel, the voice that speaks the first sentence, then the second, and so onward – call it the voice of the narrator – has, to begin with, no authority at all. Authority must be earned; on the novelist author lies the onus to build up, out of nothing, such authority. No one is better at building up authority than Tolstoy. In this sense of the word, Tolstoy is the exemplary author.

Announcements of the death of the author and of authorship made by Roland Barthes and Michel Foucault a quarter of a century ago came down to the claim that the authority of the author has never amounted to anything more than a bagful of rhetorical tricks. Barthes and Foucault took their cue from Diderot and Sterne, who long ago made a game of exposing the impostures of authorship.

There she stood, clad all in white, eyes cast down, arms clasped over her breast. My dearest Anya, I said, how happy I am to see you!; and I stood aside, careful not to stretch out a hand in case, like a shy bird, she should take flight again. Am I forgiven?

Rats. It is not as if I care for rats. Not even for dogs and cats, in the abstract. And it is not as if Señor C, cavorting up in heaven with his new wings and his harp, will care what is happening to his ex bank account. Nevertheless. Nevertheless, something bad is going on between Alan and me. I free myself from his arms and face him. Is this your true face, Alan? I say. Answer me seriously. Is this the kind of person you truly are? Because –

The Russian formalist critics of the 1920s, from whom Barthes in particular learned much, concentrated their efforts on exposing Tolstoy, above all other writers, as a rhetorician. Tolstoy became their exemplary target because Tolstoy's storytelling seemed so natural, that is to say, concealed its rhetorical artistry so well.

As a child of my times, I read, admired, and imitated Diderot and Sterne. But I never gave up reading Tolstoy, nor could I ever persuade myself that his effect on me was just a consequence of his rhetorical skill. I read him with an uneasy, even shamefaced absorption, just as (I now believe) the formalist critics who held sway in the twentieth century continued in their spare time to read the masters of realism: with guilty fascination (Barthes' own anti-theoretical theory of the pleasure of reading was, I suspect, put together to explain and justify the obscure pleasure that Zola gave him). Now that the dust has settled, the mystery of Tolstoy's authority, and of the authority of other great authors, remains untouched.

It is not a question of forgiveness, she said, still avoiding my eyes.

He interrupts me. He does not shout, but there is a quiver in his voice as if he is having to hold himself back. Anya, I am dropping the idea here and now, he says. That is the end of it. No more discussion. It was only an idea, and now it is over. Nothing has happened. He takes my hands, pulls me closer, looks me deep in the eyes. I will do anything for you, Anya, he says. I love you. Do you believe me?

During his later years, Tolstoy was treated not only as a great author but as an authority on life, a wise man, a sage. His contemporary Walt Whitman endured a similar fate. But neither had much wisdom to offer: wisdom was not what they dealt in. They were poets above all; otherwise they were ordinary men with ordinary, fallible opinions. The disciples who swarmed to them in quest of enlightenment look sadly foolish in retrospect.

What the great authors are masters of is authority. What is the source of authority, or of what the formalists called the authority-effect? If authority could be achieved simply by tricks of rhetoric, then Plato was surely justified in expelling poets from his ideal republic. But what if authority can be attained only by opening the poet-self to some higher force, by ceasing to be oneself and beginning to speak vatically?

The god can be invoked, but does not necessarily come. *Learn to speak without authority*, says Kierkegaard. By copying Kierkegaard's words here, I make Kierkegaard into an authority. Authority cannot be taught, cannot be learned. The paradox is a true one.

I said I would type your book for you, and I always do what I say.

I nod. But it is not true. I only half believe him. I believe him only half. The other half is darkness. The other half is a dark hole into which one of us is falling, I hope not me.

Say it aloud, he says. Say it properly. Do you believe me?

I believe you, I say, and I let him take me in his arms again.

*

31. On the afterlife

One way of dividing up the world's religions is into those that regard the soul as an enduring entity and those that do not. In the former, the soul, that which the I calls "I," continues to exist as itself after the body dies. In the latter, the "I" ceases to exist as itself and is absorbed into some greater soul.

Christianity gives only the most tentative account of the life of the soul after the death of the body. The soul will be eternally in the presence of God, Christianity teaches; more than that we do not know. Sometimes we are promised that in the afterlife we will be reunited with our loved ones, but this promise has little theological backing. For the rest, there are only vague images of harps and choirs.

It is just as well that the Christian theory of the afterlife is so skimpy. The soul arrives in heaven of a man who has had a number of wives and mistresses; and each of these wives and mistresses has had a number of husbands and lovers; and each of those husbands and lovers . . . For souls in this galaxy, what will constitute reunion with their loved ones? Will the wife-soul have to spend eternity not only with her beloved husband-soul but also with the detested mistress-soul who was her husband's co-beloved in the temporal realm? Will those who loved many enjoy a richer afterlife than those who loved few; or will our loved ones be defined as those we loved on our last day on earth, and them alone? In the latter case, will those of us who spent our last day in pain and terror and loneliness without the luxury of loving or being loved face eternal solitude?

Doubtless the theologian, as theorist of the afterlife, will reply that the kind of love we will feel in the beyond is unknowable to us as we are now, just as the kind of identity we will have is unknowable, and our mode of association with other souls, therefore we might as well cease speculating. But if "I" will in the next life have a kind of existence that "I" as I am now am incapable of understanding, then Christian churches should rid themselves of the doctrine of the heavenly reward, the promise that good behaviour in the present life will be rewarded with heavenly bliss in the next: whoever I am now I will not be then.

The question of the persistence of identity is even more crucial to the theory of eternal punishment. Either the soul in hell has a memory of an earlier life – a life misspent – or it has not. If it has no such memory, then eternal damnation must seem to that soul the worst, most arbitrary injustice in the universe, proof indeed that the universe is evil. Only the memory of who I was and how I spent my time on earth will permit those feelings of infinite regret that are said to be the quintessence of damnation.

It is surprising that the notion of an individual afterlife persists in intellectually respectable versions of Christianity. It so transparently fills a lack – an incapacity to think of a world from which the thinker is absent – that religion ought simply to note such incapacity as part of the human condition and leave it at that.

The persistence of the soul in an unrecognizable form, unknown to itself, without memory, without identity, is another question entirely.

Two
Second Diary

01. A dream

A troubling dream last night.

I had died but had not left the world yet. I was in the company of a woman, one of the living, younger than myself, who had been with me when I died and understood what was happening to me. She was doing her best to soften the impact of death while shielding me from other people, people who did not care for me as I had become and wanted me to depart at once.

Despite her protectiveness, this young woman did not lie to me. She too made it clear that I could not stay; and indeed I knew that my time was short, that I had a day or two at most, that no amount of protesting and weeping and clinging could change that.

In the dream I lived through the first day of my death, listening carefully for signs that my dead body was faltering. There were the faintest flutterings of hope as I saw how well I was coping with the demands of the everyday (I was, however, careful not to exert myself).

A knock at the door yesterday morning. The supervisor, Vinnie, in his nice blue uniform. A note for you, he says. A note? I say. From the gent in 108, he says. By hand? I say. By hand, says Vinnie, who is nobody's fool. How strange, I say.

The note, which could just as well have been dropped in our letter-box or substituted with a simple telephone call, but no, Señor C does not believe in the telephone, reads: *Good news. I have just sent off the manuscript on which you and I laboured so long. Which calls for a celebration. So may I invite you and your husband to drinks and refreshments at my place tomorrow evening, Friday, around 7 pm? The excellent people from Federico's will be doing the catering. Best regards, JC. PS – I hope this is not too sudden.*

I showed the note to Alan. Shall I turn him down? I said. I can be frank with him. I have earned that. I can tell him, sorry, we will feel out of place, we won't enjoy ourselves.

Then on the second day, as I was urinating, I saw the stream turn from yellow to red, and knew then that it was all true, that this was not a dream, so to speak. A little later, as if standing outside my body, I heard myself say, "I can't eat this pasta." I pushed the plate before me aside, and knew as I did so that if I could not eat pasta I could not eat anything. In fact, the interpretation I put on my words was that my internal organs were decaying irremediably.

That was the point at which I awoke. I knew at once that I had been dreaming, that the dream had gone on for a considerable time, at the same pace as its own narration, that it was a dream about my own death, that I was lucky to be able to wake from it – *I still have time left*, I breathed to myself – but that I did not dare go back to sleep (though it was the middle of the night), since to go back would be to go back into the dream.

An intriguing idea: to write a novel from the perspective of a man who has died, who knows he has two days before he – that is, his body – caves in and begins to fester and smell, who has nothing he hopes to achieve in those two days save to live some more, whose every moment is coloured with grief. Some of the people in his world simply don't see him (he is a ghost). Some are aware of him; but he gives off an air of superfluousness, his presence irritates them, they want him to go away and let them get on with their lives.

No, replied Alan. We will go. He makes a gesture, we make a gesture in return. That is civility. That is how civility works. You have relations with people even if you don't like them.

I don't understand how you can dislike Señor C so much when you have never had a proper conversation with him.

Because I know him. I know his type. If your Señor C were made dictator for a day, his first act would be to have me put against a wall and shot. Isn't that grounds enough to dislike someone?

Why would he do that? Why would he want to shoot you?

One, a woman, has a more complicated attitude. Though she is sorry he is going, though she understands that he is passing through a crisis of farewell, she nevertheless agrees it would be best for him and everyone else if he accepted his lot and departed.

A title something like "Desolation." One holds on to the belief that someone, somewhere, loves one enough to hold on to one, keep one from being torn away. But the belief is false. All love is moderate, in the end. No one will come with one.

The story of Eurydice has been misunderstood. What the story is about is the solitariness of death. Eurydice is in hell in her grave-clothes. She believes that Orpheus loves her enough to come and save her. And indeed Orpheus comes. But in the end the love Orpheus feels is not strong enough. Orpheus leaves his beloved behind and returns to his own life.

The story of Eurydice reminds us that as of the moment of death we lose all power to elect our companions. We are whirled away to our allotted fate; by whose side we get to pass eternity is not for us to decide.

The Greek view of the afterworld strikes me as truer than the Christian vision. The afterworld is a sad and subdued place.

One, because people like me have taken over the world from people like him, and a good thing too; and two, because it will leave you without any shield from his senile lust.

Don't be silly, Alan. He wants to cuddle me on his knee. He wants to be my grandfather, not my paramour. I will tell him no. I will tell him we can't come.

No, absolutely not. We will go.

You want to go?

I want to go.

02. On fan mail

In today's mail a package, postmarked Lausanne, containing a hand-written letter some sixty pages long in the form of a journal. The writer, a woman, anonymous, starts out commending me on my novels, then becomes more critical. I understand nothing about women, she says, particularly about a woman's sexual psychology. I should restrict myself to male characters.

She recounts a memory preserved from her childhood, of her father stealthily exploring her genitals while she lies in bed pretending to be asleep. In retrospect, she says, she can see that that episode shaped her entire life, making reciprocal sexual feeling on her part impossible and planting a seed of vengefulness against men in her heart.

So we went. We expected a crowd. We expected literary Sydney. We dressed up. But when the door opened, there was Señor C in his smelly old jacket. He shook Alan by the hand. So good of you to come, he said. A discreet double peck for me, one peck per cheek. In the background, a young woman in black with a white apron and a tray, hovering. Have some champagne, said Señor C.

Three glasses. Were we the only guests?

The end of a tunnel, said Señor C to Alan. I can't tell you what a comfort and support your Anya was during that dark passage.

The writer appears to be in late middle age. There is mention of a son in his thirties, but no reference to a husband. The document is nominally addressed to me, but after the first few pages could be addressed to anyone in the universe, anyone prepared to hear her cries. I think of it as a letter in a bottle, not the first to wash up on my shore. Usually the writers (it is only women who launch these missives) claim that they write to me because my books speak directly to them; but it soon emerges that the books speak only in the way that strangers whispering together might seem to be whispering about one. That is to say, there is an element of the delusional in the claim, and of the paranoid in the mode of reading.

It's interesting when men put on a show for each other. I see it with Alan's men friends too. When Alan brings me along to some office get-together, his friends don't say, *What a knockout you've got there! What tits! What legs! Lend her to me for the night! You can have mine!* They don't say it, but that is what is flashing between them. I can't count how many veiled and not so veiled propositions I have had from Alan's so-called friends, not in front of Alan but that Alan is aware of nevertheless, at some level, because that is what I am for, that is why he buys me new clothes and takes me out; that is also why he is so hot for me afterwards, while he can still see me through other men's eyes as someone fresh and alluring and illicit.

The woman from Lausanne complains above all of loneliness. She has created a protective ritual for herself in which she retires to bed at night with music playing in the background and lies cosily reading a book, immersed in what she tells herself is bliss. Then, as she begins to reflect on her situation, bliss turns to disquiet. Is this truly the best that life affords, she asks herself – lying in bed alone with a book? Is it such a good thing to be a comfortable, prosperous citizen of a model democracy, secure in her home in the heart of Europe? Despite herself, she grows more and more agitated. She rises, dons dressing gown and slippers, and takes up her pen.

As you sow, so shall you reap. I write about restless souls, and souls in turmoil answer my call.

So Señor C, who is seventy-two and is losing fine muscle control and presumably pees in his pants, says, *What a comfort and support your Anya was!*, and Alan reads at once what it means in boys' code: *Thank you for letting your girlfriend visit me and stroke her hips before me and waft her scent under my nostrils; I dream about her, I lust after her in my senile way, what a man you must be, what a stallion, to have a woman like that!* Yes, replies Alan, she is pretty good at what she does; and Señor C picks up the innuendo at once, as he is meant to.

03. My father

The last packages arrived from their place of storage in Cape Town yesterday, mainly books I had had no place for and papers I had been reluctant to destroy.

Among them was a small cardboard box that came into my possession when my father died thirty years ago. It still has a label on it, written by the neighbour who packed up his belongings: "ZC – Miscellaneous items from drawers." It contained mementoes of his spell with the South African armed forces in Egypt and Italy during World War Two: photographs of himself with fellow soldiers, badges and ribbons, a diary broken off after a few weeks and not resumed, pencil sketches of monuments (the Great Pyramid, the Colosseum) and landscapes (the Po valley); also a collection of German propaganda pamphlets. At the bottom of the box, some scattered papers from his last years, including words scrawled on a torn-off scrap of newspaper: "can something be done Im dying".

The girl in the apron turned out to be the totality of the catering by Federico's. By the time she brought in the snacks Alan had downed two glasses of champagne, and that set the pattern for the evening. I stopped drinking early, and Señor C hardly drank at all; but over supper (roast quail with baby vegetables followed by zabaglione, except that Señor C didn't have the quail, he had a butternut and tofu tartlet) Alan made serious inroads into the shiraz.

So, Juan, he said (Juan? – it was the first time I had heard Señor C addressed that way), is there some proposition you have in mind? Proposition?

The *Nachlass* of a man who asked for little from life and received little, one who, not industrious by nature – *easygoing* might be the kindest word – nevertheless resigned himself from his middle years to a round of dull toil with little variety. One of the generation whom apartheid was designed to protect and benefit; yet how slight was his gain from it! It would take a hard heart indeed, on the Day of Judgment, to consign him to the pit of hell reserved for the slavedrivers and exploiters.

Like me, he disliked friction, flare-ups, displays of anger, preferred to get along with everyone. He never told me what he thought of me. But in his secret heart I am sure he had no very high opinion. A selfish child, he must have thought, who has turned into a cold man; and how can I deny it?

Anyhow, here he is reduced to this pitiful little box of keepsakes; and here am I, their ageing guardian. Who will save them once I am gone? What will become of them? The thought wrings my heart.

Yes, some proposition. A cosy meeting, just the three of us – you must have something in mind.

No, nothing, just a little celebration.

I spotted what was going on. Always get the other party on the back foot, that is Alan's rule number one in negotiating.

And your next book – what is it going to be?

No plans yet for a next book, Alan. I am calling a halt to operations for the time being, to regroup. Then I will see what might be possible in the future.

So you have no more use for my lady-friend here. What a pity. You and she were getting along so well. Weren't you, Anya?

04. Insh'Allah

"Under the sign of death." Why should not our every utterance come accompanied by a reminder that before too long we will have to say goodbye to this world? Conventions of discourse require that the writer's existential situation, which like everyone else's is a perilous one, and at every moment too, be bracketed off from what he writes. But why should we always bow to convention? Behind every paragraph the reader ought to be able to hear the music of present joy and future grief. *Insh'Allah.*

Alan, I said. When he is bored Alan drinks heavily, just as he used to do when he was a student, without finesse, to get smashed. I don't try to hold him back because I know it doesn't work, since it is aimed at me: I am the one who got him into this situation, so, crash-crush, I can suffer for it.

My adorable lady-friend, he went on. Who has so much time on her hands nowadays, she doesn't know what to do with it. Who really threw herself heart and soul into the work she did for you. Before you had your little contretemps. But you probably didn't notice.

I noticed it, said Señor C. Anya made a real, a tangible contribution. I appreciate it.

You trust her, don't you.

Alan, I said.

Why don't we move from the table, said Señor C. Why don't we sit down.

05. On mass emotion

The fifth and last cricket test between England and Australia ended yesterday, and England won. Among spectators at the ground (the Oval, London), and in pubs around the land, there were scenes of rejoicing, with the spontaneous singing of "Land of Hope and Glory," etc. For the present the England cricket team are national heroes, fêted on all sides. Am I alone in detecting in their behaviour before the cameras an unappealing vanity, the conceit of not very bright boys whose heads have been turned by too much adulation?

Behind this jaundiced view lies a measure of prejudice and even of confusion. Though I have entered upon my eighth decade, I have yet to work out how people manage at the same time to excel at athletic pursuits and to be morally unexceptional. That is to say, despite a lifetime's schooling in scepticism, I still seem to believe that excellence, *areté*, is indivisible. How quaint!

I saw Anya the last time on the morning after the fateful celebration when that fiancé or protector of hers or whatever he was used the evening to insult me and embarrass her. She came to apologize. She was sorry the two of them had ruined the evening, she said. Alan had got the hell in – that was the phrase she used – and once Alan got the hell in, there was no stopping him. I would have thought, I said, that if it was Alan who got the hell in then it is Alan who ought to be apologizing, not his lady-friend. Alan never apologizes, said his lady-friend. Well, I said, as a matter of semantics, can one properly apologize on behalf of someone who is not in an apologetic frame of mind? She shrugged. I came to say I am sorry, she said.

It was getting on for nine o'clock. We could decently have taken our departure. But Alan was not ready to depart. Alan was just getting into his stride. With a glass in one hand and a full wine bottle in the other, he sat down heavily in an armchair. He takes no exercise. He is only forty-two, but when he drinks he gets flushed and breathes heavily, like a man with a bad heart.

In childhood, almost as soon as I learned to throw a ball, cricket took a grip on me, not just as a game but as a ritual. That grip does not seem to have relaxed, even now. But one question baffled me from the beginning: how a creature of the kind I seemed to be – reserved, quiet, solitary – could ever become good at a game in which quite another character-type seemed to excel: matter-of-fact, unreflective, pugnacious.

Scenes of mass celebration, such as have been going on in England, give me a glimpse of what I have missed out on in life, what I excluded myself from by persisting in being the kind of creature I am: the joy of belonging to (belonging in) a mass, of being swept along on currents of mass feeling.

What a realization for someone to come to who was born in Africa, where the mass is the norm and the solitary the aberration!

As a young man, I never for a moment allowed myself to doubt that only from a self disengaged from the mass and critical of the mass could true art emerge. Whatever art has come from my hand has in one way or another expressed and even gloried in this disengagement. But what sort of art has that been, in the end? Art that is not great-souled, as the Russians would say, that lacks generosity, fails to celebrate life, lacks love.

And what of the future? I said. Are you going to stay with this man who will not apologize to me and presumably does not apologize to you?

So you should, so you should, said Alan. I mean, trust her. Do you know why? Because, unbeknown to you, she has saved you. She has saved you from the depredations (he enunciated the word syllable by syllable, as if to show how clear his mind was) of an unnamed malefactor. Who shall remain nameless. Who was going to rob you blind.

06. On the hurly-burly of politics

A few weeks ago I visited the National Library in Canberra to give a reading. As a preface to the reading I made some remarks about pending security legislation. These remarks were reproduced in garbled form on the front page of the newspaper *The Australian*. I was quoted as saying that my novel *Waiting for the Barbarians* "emerged from the South Africa of the 1970s, where the security police could come in and out and barnstorm [*sic*: the word I used was *blindfold*] and handcuff you without explaining why, and take you away to an unspecified site and do what they wanted to you." The police, I was claimed to have said, "could do what they wanted because there was no real recourse against them because special provisions of the legislation indemnified them in advance." For *real* read *legal.*

I went on to mention – but this was not reported – that any journalist who reported such a disappearance might be arrested and charged with endangering the security of the state. "All of this and much more, in apartheid South Africa," I concluded, "was done in the name of a struggle against terror. I used to think that the people who created these laws that effectively suspended the rule of law were moral barbarians. Now I know they were just pioneers, ahead of their time."

Alan and I are going to take a break from each other, she replied. A trial separation, I suppose you would call it. I am going to Townsville to spend some time with my mother. I will see how I feel when things have cooled down, whether I want to come back. I have a flight this afternoon.

Really? said C, who could not have guessed what on earth Alan was talking about; he was probably imagining a masked figure with a gun in a dark alley.

Two days later *The Australian* published a letter to the editor: if I didn't like Australia, suggested the writer, I should go back to where I came from, or, if I preferred Zimbabwe, to Zimbabwe.

I had an inkling, of course, that my remarks at the library might touch a sore point, but this response, irascible, illogical (why would anyone prefer Zimbabwe to South Africa?), heavy with bile, quite took the wind out of my sails. What a sheltered life I have led! In the rough-and-tumble world of politics, a letter like this counts as no more than a pinprick, yet me it numbs like a blow from a lead cosh.

So this is our goodbye, I said.
Yeah, this is goodbye.

But she saved you, did Anya, said Alan. She pleaded on your behalf. He is a good man, she said, his heart is in the right place, with the downtrodden and oppressed, with the voiceless ones, with the humble beasts.

07. The kiss

On the wall of a hotel room in the town of Burnie, Tasmania, a poster: the streets of Paris, 1950; a young man and young woman in the act of kissing, the moment captured in black and white by the photographer Robert Doisneau. The kiss would seem to be spontaneous. A rush of feeling has overtaken the pair in mid-stride: the woman's right arm does not (not yet) return the man's embrace but hangs free, with a curve to the elbow that is the exact converse of the swell of her breast.

Their kiss is not just one of passion: with this kiss love announces itself. One puts together the story willy-nilly. He and she are students. They spent the night together, their first night, woke up in each other's arms. Now they have lectures to attend. On the sidewalk, in the midst of the morning crowd, his heart suddenly wants to burst with tenderness. She too, she is ready to give herself to him a thousand times. And so they kiss. As for the passers-by, as for the lurking camera, they could not care less. Hence "Paris, city of love." But it could happen anywhere, that night of love, that upwelling of feeling, that kiss. It could happen even in Burnie. It could have happened in this very hotel, unnoticed and unremembered, save by the lovers.

And your career? I said. What of your career?

My career. I don't know. Maybe I will give my mother a hand for a while. She built up a model agency from scratch, now it is the biggest operation in northern Queensland. Which is good going for a girl from small-town Luzon who started out with nothing.

Alan, shut up, I said. And to C I said: Alan has had too much to drink, he is going to embarrass us all if he goes on.

Who chose this poster and hung it? *Though a mere hotelkeeper, I too believe in love, can recognize the god when I see him* – is that what its presence says?

Love: what the heart aches for.

With good looks, I said. She must have started out with good looks, at least, and a good head on her shoulders. To judge from the daughter she produced.

Yeah, she has good looks. But where do looks get you, finally?

She pleaded, and I heeded her plea, said Alan. Oops, there goes the cat, the cat is out of the bag. I heeded her plea and desisted. Yes, if the truth be told, Juan, I was the one, I was the blackguard in question who was about to rob you. But did not. Because of my lady-friend here. My adorable lady-friend with the sweet sweet cunt.

08. On the erotic life

A year before he died by his own hand, my friend Gyula spoke to me about eros as he knew it in the autumn of his days.

In his youth in Hungary, said Gyula, he had been a great womanizer. But as he grew older, though he remained as keenly receptive to feminine beauty as ever, the need to make love to women in the flesh receded. To all outward appearances he became the chastest of men.

Such outward chastity was possible, he said, because he had mastered the art of conducting a love affair through all its stages, from infatuation to consummation, wholly within his mind. How could he do that? The indispensable first step was to capture what he called a "living image" of the beloved, and make it his own. Upon this image he would then dwell, giving breath to it, until he had reached a point where, still in the realm of the imagination, he could begin to make love to this succubus of his, and eventually conduct her into the utmost transports; and this whole passionate history would remain unbeknown to the earthly original. (This same Gyula, however, also claimed that no woman can be unaware of the gaze of desire settling upon her, even in a crowded room, even if she cannot detect its source.)

We took a moment, both of us, to reflect on where looks get you.

Well, I said, any time you want a job as a book editor, let me know.

C was silent. I was silent. Alan poured himself another glass.

"Here in Batemans Bay they have banned cameras on beaches and in shopping malls," Gyula said (Batemans Bay was where he spent his last years). "They say it is to protect children from the predatory attentions of paedophiles. What are they going to do next? Put out our eyes, if we are above a certain age? Make us wear blindfolds?"

He himself had scant erotic interest in children; though he collected images (he had been a photographer by profession), he was not a pornographer. He had lived in Australia since 1957 without ever feeling at ease. Australian society was too puritanical for his tastes. "If they knew what goes on in my mind," he said, "they would crucify me. I mean," he added as an afterthought, "with real nails."

I asked him what the imaginary couplings he described were like, whether they brought him anything approaching the same satisfaction as lovemaking in the real world. And by the way, I went on, had he ever reflected that the wish to ravish women in the privacy of his thoughts might be an expression not of love but of revenge – revenge upon the young and the beautiful for disdaining an ugly old man like him (we were friends, we could talk like that).

So that was what I was, a book editor, she said. I didn't know. I thought I was just a humble typist.

On the contrary, I said, on the contrary.

But that is all over, said Alan. A closed chapter. What did you say your next project was going to be, Juan?

It is not decided yet.

He laughed. "What do you think it means to be a womanizer?" he said (it was one of his favourite words in English, he liked to roll it on his tongue, *wo-man-i-zer*). "A womanizer is a man who breaks you up and makes you come together again like a woman. Like an a-tom-i-zer that breaks you up into atoms. It is only men who hate womanizers, from jealousy. Women appreciate a womanizer. A woman and a womanizer belong naturally together."

"Like a fish and a hook," I said.

"Yes, like a fish and a hook," he said. "God made us for each other."

I asked him to say more about his technique.

It all hinged, he replied, on being able to capture, through the closest, most dedicated attention, that unique unconscious gesture, too slight or too fleeting to be noticed by the average eye, by which a woman gave herself away – gave away her erotic essence, that is to say, her soul. The way she turned her wrist to look at her wristwatch, for example, or the way she reached down to pull tight the strap of a sandal. Once that unique movement was caught, the erotic imagination could explore it at leisure until the woman's every last secret was laid open, not excluding how she moved in the arms of a lover, how she came to her climax. From the giveaway gesture all followed "as if by fate."

By the way, she said, you haven't put me in your book, have you, and I don't know about it? I wouldn't like it if I was there all the time and you didn't tell me.

Ah yes, you were going to regroup, I remember. And had no more use for my lady-friend, for the time being. You know, Juan, you are the first man I have met who has tried to persuade me he has no use for Anya. Usually men can think of all kinds of uses for Anya, most of them unmentionable in polite society. But rest assured, when you say you have no use for her, I believe you.

He described his procedures to me with great candour, but not, it seemed to me, in the spirit of one offering a lesson to be followed. He had no great opinion of my eye, for women or essential gestures or anything else. Born on a savage continent, I was barred, in his opinion, from what came naturally to Europeans, namely a Greek, that is to say Platonic, turn of mind.

"You did not answer my original question," I said. "Do these masturbatory conquests of yours bring you true satisfaction? In your heart of hearts would you not prefer the real thing?"

He drew himself up. "Masturbation is a word I never use," he said. "Masturbation is for children. Masturbation is for the beginner practising his instrument. As for the real thing, how can you, who have read Freud, use that term so irresponsibly? What I speak of is ideal love, poetic love, but on the sensual plane. If you refuse to understand that, I cannot help you."

You mean in one of my opinions? What opinion do you think I might have wanted to express about you?

Not about me by name, necessarily, but about little Filipina typists who think they know everything.

Anya tells me you are very well-behaved. *Galant* certainly, but nothing more than that. No indecent whispers. No improper use of the hands. A real old-fashioned gentleman, in fact. I like that. I wish we had more like you. I am not *galant* myself. You must have noticed that. I am not a gentleman of any description. I don't even know who my parents were, who fathered me or mothered me, and you can't be a gentleman if you don't know your parents, can you?

He misjudged me. I had every reason to get a grasp of this phenomenon that he called ideal love on the sensual plane, every reason to get a grasp of it and take it over and practise it on my own behalf. But I could not. There was the real thing, which I knew and remembered, and then there was the kind of mental rape Gyula performed, and the two were not the same. The quality of the emotional experience might be similar, the ecstasy might be as intense as he averred – who was I to dispute that? – yet in the most elementary of senses a mental love could not be a real thing.

Why is it that we – men and women both, but men most of all – are prepared to accept the checks and rebuffs of the real, more and more rebuffs as time goes by, more humiliating each time, yet keep coming back? The answer: because we cannot do without the real thing, the real real thing; because without the real we die as if of thirst.

She had been in a bad mood when I opened the door to her (she was not going to stay, she had just come to apologize . . .), but already that was lightening. A few more strokes on her petals and she would begin to glow again with her wonted colour.

Didn't Anya tell you about my background? No? I was brought up in a boys' home in Queensland. I am their one success story, the one inmate who went out into the world and made his fortune legitimately. A self-made man, therefore. Do you know what I am worth, Señor Juan? Not as much as you – I am guessing, of course, how would I know how much you are worth? – but a lot nevertheless. A packet. And do you know where I keep it? No?

09. On ageing

My hip gave such pain that today I could not walk and could barely sit. Inexorably, day by day, the physical mechanism deteriorates. As for the mental apparatus, I am continually on the qui vive for broken cogs, blown fuses, hoping against hope that it will outlast its corporeal host. All old folk become Cartesians.

No opinions about typists, I said. But yes, you are in the book – how could you not be when you were part of the making of it? You are everywhere in it, everywhere and nowhere. Like God, though not on the same scale.

I keep it here. He tapped the side of his head. I keep it here. Convertible resources, I call it. Resources I can convert in a flash, I just have to make the decision. Not unlike you, I suppose. You probably store up resources in your head too, stories, plots, characters, that sort of thing. But in your line of work it takes time to realize your resources, months and years. Whereas with me it is like that – he snapped his fingers – and it is done. What do you think?

10. Idea for a story

A famous woman novelist is invited to some university or other to give a reading. Her visit coincides with the visit of Professor X, there to give a talk on (say) Hittite coinage and what it can tell us about Hittite civilization.

On a whim, the novelist attends Professor X's talk. There are only six other people in the audience. What X has to say is interesting in itself, but his delivery is monotonous and there are moments when her mind wanders. She even nods off briefly.

Later she gets into conversation with X's academic host. X, she discovers, is highly esteemed among fellow scholars; yet whereas she is being put up in a fancy hotel, X is bunking down on the couch in his host's living room. With embarrassment she realizes that while she herself is part of a modestly flourishing wing of the entertainment industry, X belongs to a neglected and disparaged company within the academy: leftovers from the bad old days, scholar-drones who bring in neither money nor kudos.

Will you send me a copy?

I will keep a copy for you. You can come and fetch it. But it will be in German, remember.

Silence. Be quiet and he will grow bored, I told myself, like one of those wind-up ducks that waddle for a while and then run down.

Her own talk, the next day, draws a large audience. In her introductory remarks she contrasts the warm welcome accorded her with the cool welcome accorded X (whom she leaves nameless). The disparity strikes her as shameful, she says; what have universities become?

At the dinner in her honour after the reading she is surprised to find that the dean, far from being upset by her remarks, is pleased. All controversy is good controversy, he tells her, all publicity good publicity. As for X, old-style scholars like him are not as badly off as she seems to think. They enjoy sheltered employment and substantial salaries, and in return for what? For pursuing researches that in the larger scheme of things amount to no more than antiquarian hobbies. Where but in public-spirited universities would they get as good a deal?

Back at home, she writes to Professor X, recounting her conversation with the dean. X writes back: You shouldn't feel bad, he says, I didn't go into Hittite studies to become rich or famous. As for you, he says, you deserve whatever has come to you, you have the divine spark.

That doesn't matter. Just as a memento. I must go now. I've got to pack.

Alan is not upset that you are leaving? He won't be lonely?

Signorina Federico appeared with coffee. She must have overheard every word from the kitchen. What Alan said about me and my private parts. Which will be closed and locked to him from this night onward. Alan paid her no attention. Not pretty enough for him.

The divine spark, she ruminates to herself: when did I last have a divine spark? She wonders what her real reason was for writing to X. Perhaps she was simply trying to excuse herself for falling asleep during his talk (he must surely have noticed).

It would make a perfectly viable story, of a minor kind. But I doubt I will ever get down to writing it. Of late, sketching stories seems to have become a substitute for writing them. I think of Gyula and his harem of images. Is it one of the consequences of growing old that one no longer needs the thing itself, that the idea of the thing suffices – as, in matters of the heart, the entertainment of a possibility, called ideal love by Gyula but more familiar to ordinary people as flirtation, may become a substitute, a not unwelcome substitute, for love itself?

Alan does not get lonely. And if he does, he can come and see me. He can come up for a weekend.

So you haven't fought, you and he. You haven't done anything irretrievable.

You know who the nameless malefactor was who nearly divested you of your capital? he pressed on. Want to guess?

You told me, said C: you.

11. *La France moins belle*

The region of France in which I am most at home is the Languedoc, where for some years I had a secondary residence. The Languedoc is by no means the most attractive part of *la belle France*. Inland the climate is unkind – stiflingly hot in summer, icy in winter. The village upon which I descended out of nowhere was undistinguished, the natives unwelcoming. Nevertheless, over the course of years the house I acquired there burrowed its way if not into my affections then into a more mysterious faculty: my sense of obligation. For a long time after I had given up the annual visits and sold the little house, *jolie* on the outside but rather sombre inside, rather cheerless, I felt a deep sadness. What would become of it now that I would no longer be there to watch over it, take care of it?

No, we don't fight. We are not children. I told him I need some fresh air, that is all. He probably needs some fresh air himself. Goodbye. Stay well. Remember: Keep out of hospitals. Hospitals make you sick.

Right. And the beauteous Anya stopped me, Anya with her heart of gold. He is my boss, she pleaded, he treats me good, how can I deceive him? She has a soft spot for you, Juan, do you know that?

The joys of possession I have never felt very acutely. I find it hard to think of myself as the owner of anything. But I do tend to slip into the role of guardian and protector of the unloved and unlovable, of what other people disdain or spurn: bad-tempered old dogs, ugly pieces of furniture that have stubbornly stayed alive, cars on the edge of breakdown. It is a role I resist; but every now and then the mute appeal of the unwanted overwhelms my defences.

A preface to a story that will never be written.

She offered me her cheek. Ever so lightly – I had not shaved, I did not want to offend – I touched my lips to that smooth skin.

Alan, I said. I gave the girl a glance; she left the room, shutting the kitchen door softly behind her.

12. The classics

I cast my mind back over the new fiction I have read in the past twelve months, trying to find one book that has truly touched me, and come up blank. For that deep touch I am driven back to the classics, to episodes that in a bygone age would have been called touchstones, stones that one would touch to renew one's faith in humanity, in the continuity of the human story: Priam kissing the hands of Achilles, pleading for the body of his son; Petya Rostov shivering with excitement as he waits to mount his horse on the morning he will die.

Even at a first reading, one has a premonition that on this misty autumn morning all will not go well for young Petya. The touches of foreshadowing that create the mood are easy enough to brush in, once we have been taught how, but from Tolstoy's pen the whole thing nevertheless emerges, time after time, miraculously fresh.

She drew back slowly, gave me a long, reflective look. Her brow furrowed. Do you want a hug? she said. And when I did not reply, she said: Seeing that I am going away, and we may not see each other again, would you like to give me a hug? So you won't forget afterwards what I was like? And, while not exactly stretching out her arms to me, she half-raised them at her sides, so that I needed to take but a single step forward to be enfolded.

She calls you Señor C, said Alan. Señor C the Senior Citizen. That is her private name for you. What about you? Do you have a private name for her? No? Not going to reveal it to me?

Petya Rostov, says my reader, his face, her face unknown to me and never to be known – *I don't remember Petya Rostov,* and goes to the shelf and takes down *War and Peace* and hunts for the death of Petya. Another of the meanings of "the classic": to be on the shelf waiting to be taken down for the thousandth, the millionth time. The classic: the perduring. No wonder publishers are so eager to claim classic status for their authors!

Thus we stood for a moment. *Behold, who can tell the workings of the Lord,* I thought to myself. At the back of my mind there was a line of Yeats too, though I could not pin down the words, only the music. Then I took the required step forward and embraced her, and for a whole minute we stood clasped together, this shrunken old man and this earthly incarnation of heavenly beauty, and could have continued for a second minute, she would have permitted that, being generous of herself; but I thought, *Enough is enough,* and let her go.

*

Anya tells me she is a bit disappointed in the way your book turned out. Tells me so in confidence. I hope you don't mind.

13. On the writing life

During the years I spent as a professor of literature, conducting young people on tours of books that would always mean more to me than to them, I would cheer myself up by telling myself that at heart I was not a teacher but a novelist. And indeed, it was as a novelist rather than as a teacher that I won a modest reputation.

But now the critics voice a new refrain. At heart he is not a novelist after all, they say, but a pedant who dabbles in fiction. And I have reached a stage in my life when I begin to wonder whether they are not right – whether, all the time I thought I was going about in disguise, I was in fact naked.

In public life the role I play nowadays is that of distinguished figure (distinguished for what no one can quite recall), the kind of notable who is taken out of storage and dusted off to say a few words at a cultural event (the opening of a new hall in the art gallery; the prize-giving at an eisteddfod) and then put back in the cupboard. An appropriately comic and provincial fate for a man who half a century ago shook the dust of the provinces off his feet and sallied forth into the great world to practise *la vie bohème*.

The truth is, I was never a bohemian, not then and not now. At heart I have always been a sobrietarian, if such a word exists, and moreover a believer in order, in orderliness. One of these days some state official or other will pin a ribbon on my shrunken chest and my reassimilation into society will be complete. *Homais, c'est moi.*

After long silence, a letter from Anya, from Brisbane.
Ola Señor!

I hope you aren't hurt. Anya is not a political animal, as you must have noticed. Your opinings on political affairs did not really engage her, she says. She was hoping for something more personal, something more toothsome. As for me, normally I don't have time for books. Too much else to occupy myself with.

"I don't see [inspiration] as a state of grace," writes Gabriel García Márquez, "nor as a breath from heaven, but as the moment when, by tenacity and control, you are at one with your theme . . . You spur the theme on and the theme spurs you on too . . . All obstacles fade away, all conflict disappears, things you never dreamt of occur to you and, at that moment, there is absolutely nothing in the world better than writing."[8]

Once or twice in a lifetime I have known the flight of the soul that García Márquez describes. Perhaps such flights do indeed come as a reward for tenacity, though I think *steady fire* better describes the needed quality. But however we name it, I no longer have it.

I read the work of other writers, read the passages of dense description they have with care and labour composed with the purpose of evoking imaginary spectacles before the inner eye, and my heart sinks. I was never much good at evocation of the real, and have even less stomach for the task now. The truth is, I have never taken much pleasure in the visible world, don't feel with much conviction the urge to recreate it in words.

As you see, I still can't call you by your first name, even if you are not Spanish at all. In my thoughts, in those days in the Towers, you were always El Señor, though I knew you wanted to move to a more personal basis. Which is a roundabout way of saying, I suppose, that to me you belong to another generation and another world, and I don't mean the world of my parents (I tried sometimes to imagine you and my mother together, but I could not even get the two of you in the same frame). Which is a roundabout way of saying something else, which I don't need to say, because I am sure you understand.

But I took this latest effort of yours seriously. We discussed it chapter by chapter, Anya and I, section by section, opinion by opinion. Took it apart. I made some observations to her and she made some observations to me. What is our verdict, you ask?

Growing detachment from the world is of course the experience of many writers as they grow older, grow cooler or colder. The texture of their prose becomes thinner, their treatment of character and action more schematic. The syndrome is usually ascribed to a waning of creative power; it is no doubt connected with the attenuation of physical powers, above all the power of desire. Yet from the inside the same development may bear a quite different interpretation: as a liberation, a clearing of the mind to take on more important tasks.

The classic case is that of Tolstoy. No one is more alive to the real world than the young Leo Tolstoy, the Tolstoy of *War and Peace*. After *War and Peace*, if we follow the standard account, Tolstoy entered upon a long decline into didacticism that culminated in the aridity of the late short fiction. Yet to the older Tolstoy the evolution must have seemed quite different. Far from declining, he must have felt, he was ridding himself of the shackles that had enslaved him to appearances, enabling him to face directly the one question that truly engaged his soul: how to live.

Anyhow, now that that is out of the way, thank you for sending me your book, which I can't read, of course, but you know that, and thank you particularly for sending the pieces you did not include in the book, which luckily I can. I know what you mean when you say they are not proper Strong Opinions, but they are my favourites anyway. I call them your Soft Opinions – I hope you don't mind.

Let me see how to put it. Our verdict, our joint verdict, comes in two parts. First part, we think you have a somewhat naïve, somewhat over-optimistic view of human nature.

14. On the mother tongue

Does each of us have a mother tongue? Do I have a mother tongue? Until recently I accepted without question that, since English is the language I command best, English must count as my mother tongue. But perhaps it is not so. Perhaps – is this possible? – I have no mother tongue.

For at times, as I listen to the words of English that emerge from my mouth, I have a disquieting sense that the one I hear is not the one I call *myself.* Rather, it is as though some other person (but who?) were being imitated, followed, even mimicked. *Larvatus prodeo.*

Writing is a less unsettling experience. Sitting in silence here, moving my hand, calling up these English words, shifting them around, substituting one for another, weaving them into phrases, I feel at ease, in control. A scene comes back from a visit to a Moscow department store: a woman working an abacus, head still, eyes still, fingers flying.

I suppose I ought to feel jealous of the someone else who took over from me and typed them for you, but I am not. I wish you happiness, and I hope your book comes out in English soon, and is a great success in the bookshops.

Contrary to what you prefer to believe, life really is a struggle. It is a struggle of all against all, and it goes on all the time. It is going on in this room at this moment. Can you deny it? Anya struggling to save you from me and my voracious depredations. You struggling to split Anya off from me. Me struggling to cut you down to size.

At the end of a day of writing-work I emerge with pages of what I am accustomed to call *what I wanted to say*. But in more cautious spirit I now ask myself: Are these words, printed out on paper, truly what I wanted to say? Is it ever good enough, as a phenomenological account, to say that somewhere deep inside I knew what I wanted to say, after which I searched out the appropriate verbal tokens and moved them around until I had succeeded in saying what I wanted to say? Would it not be more accurate to say that I fiddle with a sentence until the words on the page "sound" or "are" right, and then stop fiddling and say to myself, "That must be what you wanted to say"? If so, who is it who judges what sounds or does not sound right? Is it necessarily I ("I")?

Would the whole experience be any different, any less complicated, any better, if I were more deeply sunk, by birth and upbringing, in the language I write – in other words, if I had a truer, less questionable mother tongue than English in which to work?

Sometimes I blush when I think of the comments I made about your opinions – you were the world-famous author, after all, and I was just the little secretary – but then I think to myself, *Maybe he appreciated having a perspective from below, so to speak, an opinion of his opinions.* Because I did feel that you were taking a risk, being so isolated, so out of touch with the modern world.

You are a bit of a dreamer, Juan. A dreamer but a schemer too. We are both schemers, you and I (Anya isn't a schemer at all), but at least I don't pretend. I am a schemer because I would be devoured alive if I wasn't, by the other beasts of the jungle. And you are a schemer because you pretend to be what you are not.

Perhaps it is so that all languages are, finally, foreign languages, alien to our animal being. But in a way that is, precisely, inarticulate, inarticulable, English does not feel to me like a resting place, a home. It just happens to be a language over whose resources I have achieved some mastery.

My case can certainly not be unique. Among middle-class Indians, for example, there must be many who have done their schooling in English, who routinely speak English in the workplace and at home (throwing in the odd local locution for colouring), who command other languages only imperfectly, yet who, as they listen to themselves speak or as they read what they have written, have the uneasy feeling that there is something false going on.

I remember you once told me you would not put your dreams in the book because dreams don't count as opinions, so it is good to see one of your soft opinions is a dream, the dream you told me long ago about yourself and Eurydice. Naturally I wonder if it doesn't contain a secret message about needing help. It is a pity you are so alone in the world. We can all do with someone by our side, to help us.

You put yourself forward as a lone voice of conscience speaking up for human rights and so forth, but I ask myself, If he really believes in these human rights, why isn't he out in the real world fighting for them? What is his track record? And the answer, according to my researches, is: His track record is not so hot. In fact his track record is virtually blank.

15. On Antjie Krog

Over the airwaves yesterday, poems by Antjie Krog read in English translation by the author herself. Her first exposure, if I am not mistaken, to the Australian public. Her theme is a large one: historical experience in the South Africa of her lifetime. Her capacities as a poet have grown in response to the challenge, refusing to be dwarfed. Utter sincerity backed with an acute, feminine intelligence, and a body of heart-rending experience to draw upon. Her answer to the terrible cruelties she has witnessed, to the anguish and despair they evoke: turn to the children, to the human future, to ever-self-renewing life.

No one in Australia writes at a comparable white heat. The phenomenon of Antjie Krog strikes me as quite Russian. In South Africa, as in Russia, life may be wretched; but how the brave spirit leaps to respond!

Alan used to say you were sentimental. I never saw that. A sentimental socialist, he called you. It was meant as a put-down, of course. I never really listened when Alan ranted on about you. He thought you had undue influence on me, which was why he disliked you. I am sure that is not news to you.

So I ask myself, What is he really up to in this book of his? *Read these pages*, you tell my lady-friend (my lady-friend, not yours), looking soulfully into her eyes, *and tell me what you think of them*: what does that add up to? Shall I tell you what I have decided?

16. On being photographed

In Javier Marías's book *Written Lives* there is an essay on photographs of writers. Among the photographs reproduced is one of Samuel Beckett sitting in the corner of a bare room. Beckett looks wary, and indeed Marías describes his look as "hunted." The question is, hunted, hounded by what or whom? The most obvious answer: hounded by the photographer. Did Beckett really decide of his own free will to sit in a corner, at the intersection of three dimensional axes, gazing upward, or did the photographer persuade him to sit there? In such a position, subjected to ten or twenty or thirty flashes of the camera, with a figure crouching over you, it is hard not to feel hunted.

The fact is that photographers arrive for a shooting session with some preconception, often of a clichéd sort, of what kind of person their subject is, and strive to substantiate that cliché in the photographs they take (or, to follow the idiom of other languages, the photographs they make). Not only do they pose their subject as the cliché dictates, but when they return to their studio they select from among their shots those that come closest to the cliché. Thus we arrive at a paradox: the more time the photographer has to do justice to his subject, the less likely it is that justice will be done.

I must say I did a double take the first time you called yourself an anarchist. I thought anarchists dressed in black and tried to blow up the Houses of Parliament. You seem a very quiet kind of anarchist, very respectable.

I have decided it adds up to you wanting to get your hands on my beauteous lady-friend, but being afraid to make a move in case you get a well-deserved slap across the face. It adds up to courtship of a particularly devious kind. *From the outside I may seem withered and repulsive,* you say to her (no mention of the way you smell), *but inside I still have the feelings of a man.* Am I right? Am I right, Anya?

17. On having thoughts

If I were pressed to give my brand of political thought a label, I would call it pessimistic anarchistic quietism, or anarchist quietistic pessimism, or pessimistic quietistic anarchism: anarchism because experience tells me that what is wrong with politics is power itself; quietism because I have my doubts about the will to set about changing the world, a will infected with the drive to power; and pessimism because I am sceptical that, in a fundamental way, things can be changed. (Pessimism of this kind is cousin and perhaps even sister to belief in original sin, that is, to the conviction that humankind is imperfectible.)

But do I really qualify as a thinker at all, someone who has what can properly be called thoughts, about politics or about anything else? I have never been easy with abstractions or good at abstract thought.

Did you have undue influence on me? I don't think so. I don't think you had much influence on me at all. I don't mean that in a negative way. I was lucky to meet you when I did. I would probably still be with Alan but for you; but you didn't influence me. I was myself before I met you and I am still myself now, no change.

I stood up. Time to go home, Alan, I said. Thank you, Mister C, for including us in your celebration. I am sorry we spoiled it, but it is nothing serious, nothing to take to heart, it will all blow over, Alan has just had a little too much to drink.

In the course of a lifetime's mental activity, the one and only idea I have had that might count as abstract came to me late, in my fifties, when it dawned on me that certain everyday mathematical concepts might help clarify moral theory. For moral theory has never quite known what to do with quantity, with numbers. Is killing two people worse than killing one person, for example? If so, how much worse? Twice as bad? Not quite twice as bad – one and a half times as bad, say? Is stealing a million dollars worse than stealing one dollar? What if that one dollar is the widow's mite?

Questions like these are not merely scholastic. They must exercise the minds of judges every day, as they ruminate on what fine to impose, what term of imprisonment to set.

The idea that came to me was simple enough, though cumbersome when put in words. In mathematics, a wholly ordered set is a set of elements in which each element has to stand either to the left of or to the right of each other element. Where numbers are concerned, *to the left of* can be interpreted to mean less than, *to the right of* to mean greater than. The integers (whole numbers), positive and negative, are an example of a wholly ordered set.

You opened my eyes somewhat, I will say that. You showed me there was another way of living, having ideas and expressing them clearly and so forth. Of course you need to have talent to make a success of that. It is not something I could do. But maybe, in another life, if our ages were more compatible, you and I could set up house together and I could be your inspiration. Your resident inspiration. How would you like that? You could sit at your desk and write, and I could take care of the rest.

You have forgotten the second part, said Alan. Sit down, dear, I haven't told Juan the second part of our verdict.

In a set that is only partially ordered, the requirement that any given element must be *either* to the right of *or* to the left of any other given element does not hold.

In the realm of moral judgments, we can think of *to the left of* as worse than, *to the right of* as better than. If we treat the set of elements about which we wish to come to a moral judgment as constituting not a wholly ordered set but a partially ordered set, then there will be pairs of elements (a single victim as against two victims; a million dollars as against a mite) to which the ordering relation, the moral question *better or worse?*, does not necessarily apply. In other words, the unrelieved *better or worse?* line of questioning has simply to be abandoned.

The presumption that any and every set of elements can be ordered leads, in the realm of moral questions, straight into a quagmire. Which is worse, the death of a bird or the death of a human child? Which is worse, the death of an albatross or the death of an insentient, brain-damaged infant hooked up to a life-support machine?

Pay no attention. Just an idea.

I am actually quite a practical person. You never saw that side of me, but it's true. A practical person but not a dreamer, unfortunately. So if it is a fellow dreamer you are looking for, a dreamer who will also wash your underwear and cook you fabulous meals, you will have to keep looking, I am not the one for you.

In reaching part two of our verdict, we deliberated as follows, Anya and I. He is handing down a set of pronouncements on the modern world, we said to ourselves, but aimed at a German public. Isn't that a little odd – to be writing a book in English for a bunch of Krauts? How are we to explain it?

Unfortunately, the intuitive appeal of ordered-set thinking makes it hard to relinquish. This is particularly evident in jurisprudence. Trying to produce a sentence harsher ("worse") than death to pronounce upon Adolf Eichmann, his Israeli judges came up with: "You shall be hanged and your body shall be burnt to ash and the ash shall be scattered outside the boundaries of Israel." But in this double sentence – upon Eichmann and then upon his mortal remains – there is more than a hint of desperation. Death is absolute. There is no worse; and this is so not only for Eichmann but for each of the six million Jews who died at the hands of the Nazis. Six million deaths are not the same as – do not "add up to," in a certain sense do not "exceed" – one death ("merely" one death); nevertheless, what does it mean – what *exactly* does it mean – to say that six million deaths are, in ensemble, worse than one death? It is not a paralysis of the faculty of reason that leaves us staring helplessly at the question. It is the question itself that is at fault.

I have been thinking about your friend the Hungarian photographer and what he told you. Most of the photographers I have worked with have been gay, that is how it is in the fashion world, but still, when a camera is pointed at me I know I move differently, it does not matter who is behind it. In fact it is more than that, more than just the way I move. I almost seem to be standing outside myself, observing what I look like to the camera. It is like seeing yourself in a mirror, only more so, because it is not your eyes that are doing the seeing, but someone else's.

The explanation we came up with is the following. That in the English-speaking world, the world of hard heads and common sense, a book of pronouncements on the real world won't get much traction, coming from a man whose sole achievement lies in the sphere of the fanciful.

18. On the birds of the air

Once upon a time the little strip of land across from the Towers belonged to the birds, who scavenged in the creek bed and cracked open pine cones for the kernels. Now it has become a green space, a public park for two-legged animals: the creek has been straightened, concreted over, and absorbed into the runoff network.

From these new arrivals the birds keep a cautious distance. All save the magpies. All save the magpie-in-chief (that is how I think of him), the oldest – at least the stateliest and most battered looking. He (that is how I think of him, male to the core) walks in slow circles around me where I sit. He is not inspecting me. He is not curious about me. He is warning me, warning me off. He is also looking for my vulnerable point, in case he needs to attack, in case it comes down to that.

My guess is your friend had his fantasies about girls while he was photographing them. At least it sounds to me like a photographer's thing. I never used to think about what was going on in the photographer's mind while he was doing his job. I mean I deliberately never thought about it. It would spoil the picture, make it lewd, in a way, if the model and the photographer were in collusion, or so it seemed to me. Be yourself, I used always to whisper to myself, meaning I should just sink away into myself, like into a pond, without ripples.

Whereas in places like Germany and France people still tend to drop to their knees before sages with white beards. Tell us, O Master, we pray, what has gone wrong with our civilization! Why have the wells run dry, why is there a rain of frogs? Look into your mystic ball and enlighten us! Show us the road to the future!

At the end of the road (this is how I conceive it) he is prepared to entertain the possibility of a compromise: a compromise, for example, in which I beat a retreat into one of the protective cages that we human animals have erected on the far side of the street, while he retains this space as his own; or a compromise in which I agree to come out of my cage only during specified hours, between three and five in the afternoon, say, when he likes to take a snooze.

One morning there was a sudden imperious clatter at my kitchen window. There he was, clinging to the ledge with his claws, slapping his wings, glaring in, serving me with a warning: even indoors I might not be safe.

Now, in late spring, he and his wives sing to each other all night in the treetops. They could not care less that they keep me awake.

The magpie-in-chief has no firm idea of how long human beings live, but he thinks it is not as long as magpies. He thinks I will die in that cage of mine, die of old age. Then he can batter the window down, strut in, and peck out my eyes.

Every now and again, when the weather is hot, he deigns to drink from the bowl of the drinking fountain. In the moment when he

---

I also wonder if your Hungarian friend really exists (existed). Maybe he is just another of your stories. You need not tell me. It can be a secret of yours. But I would like to hear why he killed himself.

Anyway, whether your friend was real or not, let me own up, I never minded if you had fantasies about me. From other men I sometimes minded it, but not from you. It was one of the ways I could be of help – at least that was what I told myself.

You have decided to try your hand at being a guru, Juan. That is what we concluded, Anya and I. You took a look around the job market – this is how we pictured it to ourselves – and saw that it was tight, particularly for the over-seventies. Placards in every window: *Oldies need not apply.* But then, hello, what is this?

raises his beak to allow the water to run down his gullet, he makes himself vulnerable to attack, and he is aware of that. So he is careful to maintain a particularly severe mien. Just dare laugh, he says, and I will come after you.

I never waver from according him the full respect, the full attention he demands. This morning he caught a beetle and was very proud of himself – chuffed with himself, as the English say. With the beetle helpless in his beak, its wings broken and splayed on either side, he hopped toward me, pausing at length with each hop, until he was no more than a metre removed. "Well done," I murmured to him. He cocked his head to listen to my brief, two-syllable song. Was he acknowledging me, I asked myself? Do I come here often enough to count, in his eyes, as part of his establishment?

There are visits from the cockatoos as well. One sits peaceably in a wild plum tree. He regards me, holds out a plum kernel in his claw as if to say, "Would you like a bite?" I want to say, "This is a public garden. You are as much a visitor as I, it is not up to you to offer me food." But public, private, it is no more than a puff of air to him. "It's a free world," he says.

Let's look nice for Señor C, I used to say to myself when I was getting ready to pay you a visit in the mornings – for Señor C, who must get lonely sitting by himself all day with no one to talk to but the dictaphone and sometimes the birds. Let's look nice for him, so he can stock up on memories and have something to dream about when he goes to bed tonight.

"Wanted: Senior Guru. Must have lifetime of experience, wise words for all occasions. Long white beard a plus." Why don't I give that a shot? you said to yourself. I have not exactly been lionized as a novel-writer – let us see if they will lionize me as a guru.

19. On compassion

Every day for the past week the thermometer has risen above the forty-degree mark. Bella Saunders in the flat down the corridor tells me of her concern for the frogs along the old creek bed. Will they not be baked alive in their little earthen chambers? she asks anxiously. Can we not do something to help them? What do you suggest? I say. Can we not dig them out and bring them indoors until the heatwave is over? she says. I caution her against trying. You won't know where to dig, I say.

Toward sunset I observe her carry a plastic bowl of water across the street, which she leaves in the creek. In case the little ones get thirsty, she explains.

It is easy to make fun of people like Bella, to point out that heatwaves are part of a larger ecological process with which human beings ought not to interfere. But does this criticism not miss something? Are we human beings not part of that ecology too, and is our compassion for the wee beasties not as much an element of it as is the cruelty of the crow?

I hope you don't mind my saying this. It would have been better if you thought I was all natural, I was just being myself, I had no idea of the thoughts you were having about me. But you can't be friends if you are not going to be frank (love is a different story), and if I can't be your little typist any more at least I can be your friend. So I will tell you frankly, I was never embarrassed by your thoughts, I even helped them along a little. And nothing has changed since I left, you can go on having thoughts about me to your heart's content (that is the beauty of thoughts, isn't it, that distance doesn't matter, and separation). And if you want to write and tell me your thoughts, that is OK too, I can be discreet.

The only problem is, in the English-speaking world we take our gurus with a pinch of salt. On the sales charts, who do gurus find themselves competing with? With celebrity chefs. With actresses retailing stale gossip. With superannuated politicians.

20. On children

Another lesson from my hours in the park.

I approve of children, in the abstract. Children are our future. It is good for old people to be around children, it lifts our spirits. And so forth.

What I forget about children is the unending racket they make. Baldly put, they shout. Shouting is not simply talking writ loud and large. It is not a means of communication at all, but a way of drowning out rivals. It is a form of self-assertion, one of the purest there is, easy to practise and highly effective. A four-year-old may not be as strong as a grown man, but he certainly is louder.

One of the first things we should learn along the road toward being civilized: not to shout.

What I don't want, if you write or if you call, is news. I have put Sydenham Towers behind me, and Alan too. That's me, that's the way I am: if I am into something, I am wholly in, but if it doesn't work out, I put it behind me, it is finished, it doesn't exist any more. That way I remain positive, that way I can look to the future. So I don't want news about Alan.

Not distinguished company. So you thought to yourself, *Let us try old Europe. Let us see if old Europe will give me the kind of hearing I won't get at home.*

21. On water and fire

Heavy rainfall this week. As I watch the trickle that runs through the park turn into a torrent, the deeply alien nature of floodwater is brought home to me. The flood is not puzzled or disconcerted by obstacles or barriers it finds in its way. Puzzlement, disconcertment are not in its repertoire. Barriers are simply overrun, obstacles shoved aside. The nature of water, as the pre-Socratics might have said, is to flow. For water to be puzzled, to hesitate even for an instant, would be against its nature.

Fire is equally alien to the human. Intuitively one thinks of fire as a devouring force. Whatever devours must have an appetite, and it is in the nature of appetite to become satiated. But fire is never satiated. The more a fire devours, the bigger it gets; the bigger it gets, the more its appetite grows; the more its appetite grows, the more it devours. All that refuses to be devoured by fire is water. If water could burn, all of the world would have been consumed by fire long ago.

Did I tell you I asked Alan to send me the rest of my stuff? I asked him to ship it care of my mother. I said I would pay. That was four months ago. No reply. Silence. If I were a different kind of person I would arrive at the flat with a can of kerosene (I've still got a key) and set fire to it. Then he would know what a wronged woman is capable of. But I am not like that.

But Anya is flashing me looks, I see. We are overstaying our welcome. Dear me, I am so sorry. We must be on our way. Thank you, Juan, for a wonderful evening. Truly stimulating. Truly stimulating, don't you agree, Anya?

22. On boredom

Only the higher animals are capable of being bored, said Nietzsche. This observation must, I suppose, be taken as a compliment to Man as one of the higher animals, though a compliment of a backhanded nature: Man's mind is restless; unless it is given occupation it will become clouded with irritation, will descend into fidgetiness and even, eventually, into malicious, ill-judged destructiveness.

As a child I would seem to have been an unwitting Nietzschean. I was convinced that the boredom endemic among my contemporaries was a sign of their higher nature, that it expressed a tacit judgment on whatever it was that bored them, and therefore that whatever bored them should be looked down on for failing to meet their legitimate human needs. So when my schoolfellows were bored by poetry, for instance, I concluded that poetry itself was at fault, that my own absorption in poetry was deviant, culpable, and above all immature.

My mother says, Let him keep the stuff, it's just stuff, you can get more, it's his loss, where will he find another girl like my Anya? My mother is very loyal. That is how we are, we Filipinas. Good wives, good mistresses, good friends too. Everything good.

In the elevator I at last had a chance to say my say. For what you have made me undergo this evening I will never forgive you, Alan, I said. Never. And I mean it.

In reasoning thus I was abetted by much of the literary criticism of the day, which said that the modern age (meaning the twentieth century) demanded poetry of a new, modern cast that would break decisively with the past, in particular with the poetry of the Victorians. To the truly modern poet nothing could be more retrograde and therefore more contemptible than a liking for Tennyson.

The fact that my classmates were bored by Tennyson proved to me, if proof were needed, that they were the authentic if unconscious bearers of the new, modern sensibility. Through them the Zeitgeist pronounced its stern judgment on the Victorian age, and on Tennyson in particular. As for the troublesome fact that my classmates were equally bored (to say nothing of being baffled) by T.S. Eliot, this was to be explained by a lingering effeteness in Eliot, a failure on his part to measure up to their brusque masculine standards.

It did not occur to me that my classmates found poetry boring – as they found all their school subjects boring – because they could not concentrate.

Don't have bad thoughts about Alan. Bad thoughts can spoil your day, and is it worth it, to spoil your day, when you haven't got so many days left? Keep a tranquil mind, treat him like he doesn't exist, like he is someone in a bad story that you threw away.

In the bright light from above, Alan's jowls sagged. He looked at that moment like what he was: a surly, dissatisfied, half-drunk, middle-aged white Australian.

The most serious consequences of the non sequitur into which I had fallen (the highest intelligences are the soonest bored, therefore the soonest bored possess the highest intelligence) came in the area of religion. I found religious observances boring, therefore *a fortiori* my contemporaries, as modern spirits, had to find religion boring too. Their failure to betray symptoms of boredom, their willingness to parrot Christian doctrine and profess a Christian morality while continuing to behave like savages, I took as evidence of a mature ability on their part to live out the disjunction between the real (visible, tangible) world and the fictions of religion.

Only now, late in life, do I begin to see how ordinary people, Nietzsche's bored higher animals, really cope with their environment. They cope not by becoming irritated but by lowering their expectations. They cope by learning to sit through things, by letting the mental machinery run at a slower rate. They slumber; and because they do not mind slumbering they do not mind being bored.

We had a good relationship, you and I – don't you think?
– and it was based on honesty. We were pretty honest with
each other. I liked that. I couldn't always be honest with Alan.

Nothing, I said, nothing that I have done or that C has done justifies the way you have behaved.

To me, the failure of my teachers, the Marist Brothers, to appear each morning robed in fire and uttering deep and terrible metaphysical truths was proof that they were unworthy servants. (Servants of whom, of what? Not of God, certainly – God did not exist, I did not need to be told that – but of Truth, of Nothingness, of the Void.) To my youthful contemporaries, on the other hand, the Brothers were simply boring. They were boring because everything was boring; and since everything was boring nothing was boring, you just learned to live with it.

Since I was in flight from religion, I assumed that my classmates had to be in flight from religion too, albeit in a quieter, savvier way than I had as yet been able to discover. Only today do I realize how mistaken I was. They were never in flight at all. Nor are their children in flight, or their grandchildren. By the time I reached my seventieth year, I used to predict, all the churches in the world would have been turned into barns or museums or potteries. But I was wrong. Behold, new churches spring up every day, all over the place, to say nothing of mosques. So Nietzsche's dictum needs to be amended: While it may be so that only the higher animals are capable of boredom, man proves himself highest of all by domesticating boredom, giving it a home.

You can't be honest in a marriage-type relationship where you live together, not absolutely honest, not if you want it to last. That is one of the down things about marriage.

The door opened on the twenty-fifth floor. I hear you, said Alan. I hear you loud and clear. And do you know what I say in return, my little chickadee? I say, Get stuffed.

*

23. On J.S. Bach

The best proof we have that life is good, and therefore that there may perhaps be a God after all, who has our welfare at heart, is that to each of us, on the day we are born, comes the music of Johann Sebastian Bach. It comes as a gift, unearned, unmerited, for free.

How I would like to speak just once to that man, dead now these many years! "See how we in the twenty-first century still play your music, how we revere and love it, how we are absorbed and moved and fortified and made joyful by it," I would say. "In the name of all mankind, please accept these words of tribute, inadequate though they are, and let all you endured in those bitter last years of yours, including the cruel surgical operations on your eyes, be forgotten."

Whatever you do, don't allow yourself to get depressed. I know you believe you are not what you used to be, but the fact is you are still a good-looking man and a real gentleman too, who knows how to make a woman feel like a woman. Women appreciate that in a man, whatever else may be lacking. As for your writing, you are without a doubt one of the best, class AA, and I say that not just as your friend. You know how to draw the reader in (for example, in the bit about the birds in the park).

Long after the break-up with Alan, after the move to Queensland, after Señor C sent me his book and I wrote back to thank him, I made a call to Mrs Saunders in the Towers. I never got to know Mrs Saunders properly while I was there, she is a bit dippy (she was the one who told me Señor C was from Colombia, she must have mixed him up with someone else), but her flat is on the same floor as his and I know she has a soft heart (she was the one who used to feed the birds in the park).

Why is it to Bach and Bach alone that I have this longing to speak? Why not Schubert ("Let the cruel poverty in which you had to live be forgotten")? Why not Cervantes ("Let the cruel loss of your hand be forgotten")? Who is Johann Sebastian Bach to me? In naming him, do I name the father I would elect if, from all the living and the dead, one were allowed to elect one's father? Do I in this sense choose him as my spiritual father? And what is it that I want to make up for by bringing at last a first, faint smile to his lips? For having been, in my time, such a bad son?

You bring things to life. If I have to be honest, the strong opinions on politics and so forth were not your best, maybe because there is no story in politics, maybe because you are a bit out of touch, maybe because the style does not suit you. But I really do hope you will publish your soft opinions one day. If you do, remember to send a copy to the little typist who showed you the way.

At a personal level, things are going well in my life. I have moved to Brisbane, as you can see. Townsville was too small for me, at heart I am a city person. I am seeing a man here and we are happy together (I think). He is a regular Aussie, he has his own business (air-conditioning), and he is more my age (Alan wasn't right for me in that respect). Maybe he and I will get hooked up – we'll see. He wants children, and I have not forgotten what you advised, about not leaving it too late.

Mrs Saunders, I said, will you phone me if something happens to the Señor, if he has to go to hospital or worse? I could ask Alan, my ex, but things between the two of us are a little cool, and anyway, Alan is a man and men don't notice things. Phone me and I will come down. It is not as if I can do much for him – I am not a nurse – but I don't like to think of him all alone, facing, you know, the end. He has no children and no family that I know of, not in this country, so there won't be anyone to make the arrangements, and that is not nice, not appropriate, if you know what I mean.

24. On Dostoevsky

I read again last night the fifth chapter of the second part of *The Brothers Karamazov*, the chapter in which Ivan hands back his ticket of admission to the universe God has created, and found myself sobbing uncontrollably.

While I was in Townsville I did some modelling, just for a giggle. If you feel like it, call up www.sunseasleep.com.au – it is a mail-order catalogue, and I am in the nightwear pages, looking pretty fetching, if I say so myself. So there is always that to fall back on, until my looks desert me, which is a comfort.

I am not sure that Mrs Saunders really knew what I meant, she is somewhat otherworldly and Señor C does not figure heavily on her radar anyway, but she took down my number and promised to call.

Don't tell him, I said. Promise. Don't tell him I have been inquiring. Don't tell him I am worried.

She promised, for what that is worth.

These are pages I have read innumerable times before, yet instead of becoming inured to their force I find myself more and more vulnerable before them. Why? It is not as if I am in sympathy with Ivan's rather vengeful views. Contrary to him, I believe that the greatest of all contributions to political ethics was made by Jesus when he urged the injured and offended among us to turn the other cheek, thereby breaking the cycle of revenge and reprisal. So why does Ivan make me cry in spite of myself?

I have not heard from Alan for months. After the break-up he would phone every day, wanting me to come back. But he never actually came in person, and my test of a man's love is whether he is prepared to kneel down in front of you and offer you a bouquet of red roses and beg your forgiveness and promise to mend his ways. Pretty romantic, isn't it? Pretty unrealistic too.

Am I worried? Not really, not in the usual way. We have all got to die, he is old, he is as ready to go as he will ever be. What is the point in hanging on just for the sake of hanging on? It's OK while you can still take care of yourself, but even by the time I left Sydney I could see he was getting a bit trembly, a bit doddery. Before too long he would have to give up that flat of his and move into a home, and he would not like that. So it is not his death that concerns me so much as what may happen to him on the way there. Mrs Saunders may be the one with the soft heart, but Mrs Saunders is just a neighbour, whereas I was always a little more.

The answer has nothing to do with ethics or politics, everything to do with rhetoric. In his tirade against forgiveness Ivan shamelessly uses sentiment (martyred children) and caricature (cruel landowners) to advance his ends. Far more powerful than the substance of his argument, which is not strong, are the accents of anguish, the personal anguish of a soul unable to bear the horrors of this world. It is the voice of Ivan, as realized by Dostoevsky, not his reasoning, that sweeps me along.

Anyway, Alan never came, and I stopped answering his calls, and eventually he stopped calling. I suppose he found someone else. I don't want to know, so don't tell me. He should never have left his wife in the first place. I blame myself for that. He should have stuck it out.

I was the one he was in love with, in his old man's way, which I never minded as long as it did not go too far. I was his secret aria secretary, I used to say to him (just joking), and he never denied it. If I had cared to listen in on a warm spring night, I am sure I would have heard him crooning his love song up the lift shaft. Him and the magpie. Mr Melancholy and Mr Magpie, the amoro-dolorous duo.

Are those tones of anguish real? Does Ivan "really" feel as he claims to feel, and does the reader in consequence "really" share Ivan's feelings? The answer to the latter question is troubling. The answer is Yes. What one recognizes, even as one hears Ivan's words, even as one asks whether he genuinely believes what he says, even as one asks whether one wants to rise up and follow him and give back one's ticket too, even as one asks whether it is not mere rhetoric ("mere" rhetoric) that one is reading, even as one asks, shocked, how a Christian, Dostoevsky, a follower of Christ, could allow Ivan such powerful words – even in the midst of all this there is space enough to think too, *Glory be! At last I see it before me, the battle pitched on the highest ground! If to anyone (Alyosha, for instance) it shall be given to vanquish Ivan, by word or by example, then indeed the word of Christ will be forever vindicated!* And therefore one thinks, *Slava, Fyodor Michailovich! May your name resound for ever in the halls of fame!*

Some friendly advice, before I forget. Have a professional come in and clean your hard drive. It will cost a hundred dollars maybe, but you could end up saving yourself a packet. Look under Computer Services in the Yellow Pages.

I will fly to Sydney. I will do that. I will hold his hand. I can't go with you, I will say to him, it is against the rules. I can't go with you but what I will do is hold your hand as far as the gate. At the gate you can let go and give me a smile to show you are a brave boy and get on the boat or whatever it is you have to do. As far as the gate I will hold your hand, I would be proud to do that. And I will clean up afterwards. I will clean your flat and put everything in order. I will drop *Russian Dolls* and the other private stuff in the trash, so you don't need to have sinking thoughts on the other side about what people on this side will be saying about you. I will take your clothes to the charity shop. And I will write to the man in Germany, Mr Wittwoch, if that is his name, to let him know that is the end of your Opinions, there won't be any more coming in.

And one is thankful to Russia too, Mother Russia, for setting before us with such indisputable certainty the standards toward which any serious novelist must toil, even if without the faintest chance of getting there: the standard of the master Tolstoy on the one hand and of the master Dostoevsky on the other. By their example one becomes a better artist; and by better I do not mean more skilful but ethically better. They annihilate one's impurer pretensions; they clear one's eyesight; they fortify one's arm.

I know you get a lot of fan mail from admirers which you chuck away, but I am hoping this got through to you.
Bye,
Anya (admirer too)

All that I will promise him, and hold his hand tight and give him a kiss on the brow, a proper kiss, just to remind him of what he is leaving behind. Good night, Señor C, I will whisper in his ear: sweet dreams, and flights of angels, and all the rest.

Notes

1. Thomas Hobbes, *On the Citizen*, edited and translated by Richard Tuck (Cambridge: Cambridge University Press, 1988), chapter 10, pp. 115–16.
2. *Discours de la servitude volontaire*, sections 20, 23.
3. *Principe*, chapter 18.
4. H.S. Versnel, "Beyond Cursing: The Appeal to Justice in Judicial Prayers," in *Magika Hiera: Ancient Greek Magic and Religion*, ed. Christopher A. Faraone and Dirk Obbink (New York: Oxford University Press, 1991), pp. 68–9.
5. Jean-Pierre Vernant, "Intimations of the Will in Greek Tragedy," in Jean-Pierre Vernant and Pierre Vidal-Naquet, *Myth and Tragedy in Ancient Greece*, trans. Janet Lloyd (New York: Zone Books, 1990), p. 81.
6. "Funes the Memorious," trans. James E. Irby, in *Labyrinths*, ed. Donald A. Yates and James E. Irby (New York: New Directions, 1962), pp. 64–5.
7. Judith Brett, "Relaxed and Comfortable," *Quarterly Essay* no. 19 (2005), pp. 1–79.
8. *The Fragrance of Guava*, trans. Ann Wright (London: Verso, 1983), p. 34.

Acknowledgements

I am grateful to Cambridge University Press for permission to quote from Thomas Hobbes, *On the Citizen* (Cambridge, 1988); to Carmen Balcells and the author for permission to quote from Gabriel García Márquez, *The Fragrance of Guava* (London, 1983); to New Directions for permission to quote from Jorge Luis Borges, *Labyrinths* (New York, 1962); to Oxford University Press for permission to quote from *Magika Hiera* (New York, 1991); and to Zone Books for permission to quote from Jean-Pierre Vernant and Pierre Vidal-Naquet, *Myth and Tragedy in Ancient Greece* (New York, 1990).

For their generously given advice, my thanks to Danielle Allen, Reinhild Boehnke, Piergiorgio Odifreddi, and Rose Zwi. For what I have made of their advice I alone am responsible.

JMC